The Evolution of Confusion ...5 of 5 (We Should Know ...)

Stephen Meiner

Published by Stephen Meiner, 2023.

THE EVOLUTION OF CONFUSION ...5 OF 5 (WE SHOULD KNOW ...)

First edition. February 2, 2023.

Copyright © 2023 Stephen Meiner.

ISBN: 979-8215072752

Written by Stephen Meiner.

XXXIII.

That isn't good enough for Rebekkah. When she had initially sent them to deliver the horse, and they reported back that they couldn't find Shannon, she did not tell Cindy. She did not want to worry her. But for Murray and Sweeney—-they were not to return until they found Shannon. Then Rebekkah was furious when they told her that they had found her, but had left her on the island while they returned to get supplies from the mission base.

Sweeney had told Rebekkah that Shannon was an adult, and they couldn't tell her what to do. Sweeney had added that if Shannon could be ordered around, then she wouldn't have gone to the 'mission field' the second time. She would have listened to all the others—-inclusive of Rebekkah's persuasion.

Rebekkah isn't trying to find an avenue to blame someone. She is just frustrated. She had long struggled with the fine line between trying to control and trying to accept the fact that everything seems out-of-control. She doesn't quite have a healthy balance between what she can do, and what she should leave to prayer alone—-and the workings of God.

Sweeney has mixed feelings about sharing this latest piece of news. But he has resolved to attempt to do what is right—-from this point forward. He attempts to tell Rebekkah that Cindy's husband is alive, but she sounds angry—-as if she doesn't believe him. Yet, he anticipates she will be more so ...when she does believe him.

Rebekkah's emotions are all over the map—-literally. She can't stand the fact that they are on the opposite side of the world and everything is falling way short of her expectations. Yet, she still doesn't know how to act when things exceed her expectations either. She gets Lorvin to verify the fact that Shannon has found her Dad. Then Rebekkah tells Sweeney that if he and Murray can bring

Stephen and Shannon back home safely, she'll buy them both new ships—-the best that money can buy.

That's when Sweeney prepares himself for the response he will receive next, "Stephen is very sick. We can't guarantee he will make it out of the mission hospital, let alone the long trip back home. Yet my hope is still strong that we can deliver. But there's one more thing."

Rebekkah doesn't like it when she hears that there is one more thing, "Okay, what's that?"

Sweeney hesitates, "Well, I can't accept your offer."

Rebekkah is a bit confused about what part of her offer he is unwilling to accept, "What do you mean ...you can't accept my offer?"

Sweeney releases all that pent-up emotion. After all these years, he now tells how he is responsible for allowing everyone to think Stephen was not alive.

Sweeney can tell the silence is not the result of a problem with the phone. Rebekkah isn't saying anything—-and that is usually worse than her saying something.

Rebekkah breaks the silence, "I could get angry with you for what you just told me, but maybe I can even surprise myself this time. God had you play a part in this. I don't know yet what that all involves, but I do know God has reasons and purposes. And the fact is, if God hadn't used you, then I'd be still facing the fact that Stephen is dead. As it is, he is alive, and I'd like to celebrate with you."

Sweeney is swallowing hard, but he's relieved, "Are you okay, Rebekkah? I'm thankful for your grateful perspective, but this doesn't sound like you."

Sweeney is so right. Rebekkah is still having a difficult time restraining certain feelings. If he hadn't allowed everyone to believe that Stephen was dead, then perhaps her best friend, Stephen's mom, might still be alive today. Rebekkah needs real strength to stay on the course without sounding too coarse.

Rebekkah refers back to her only strength, "I was just reading the Book of Genesis last night. When I read how Joseph did not focus on the intent of his brothers, but rather upon understanding God's purpose, it really had an impact upon me. I haven't at all been living my life that way."

One person who would not only not see God's purpose, but seldom saw any purpose other than his own—-is Scottie. Sweeney and Murray's dad is a hard man. And most of their life, they found it preferable not to tell him the truth. If the truth did not align with his expectations, they had much reason to fear telling the truth.

But at this point, Sweeney finds it preferable to tell the truth. There is no way he can bring back to memory all those times he had not told the truth, but he can begin by confessing in general—-and at least specifically own up to this one.

Sweeney thinks back. His dad had never owned up to anything. He came closer to the concept of looking at children as ownership, instead of children of God. But still, Sweeney feels he has to try. He has to try talking to his dad.

Scottie provides more of the same of which he'd filled their childhood with, "It doesn't surprise me. Always making life so difficult for your dad. But that wasn't good enough for you, was it? You had to mess with other people's lives too, didn't you?"

Scottie's frame of mind had not changed. He is well into his regular routine, "Why are you telling me all this anyway? Like I always said, if you're going to tell a lie, don't ever admit to it. Let me talk to Murray—-you disappoint me too much."

Sweeney hands the phone to Murray, then walks off to be by himself. He had hoped dad would not affect him this way. But it doesn't matter how long it's been—-that gripping disappointment, expressed from dad to son, continues to rob him of the blessing he could now potentially realize.

****

Sweeney needs to be alone to reflect on this one. It seems just like yesterday. He and Murray sit by the window, looking out. They're always looking out. No one seems to look out for them. They are grounded again. They are grounded a lot, he recalls.

Dad is angry. Mom is angry. Don't know who was angry first. Does it really matter?

We become a part of dad and mom whether we like it or not. What will children gain from their parents? The positive, or the negative? Or the confusion?

A therapist blames upbringing ...an uncomfortable insinuation for parents, or parents of parents. Parents blame children, an unbearable insinuation for children. Children don't have the right to blame anyone, unless they blame themselves. They're just the unwilling victims of it all. And many of the supposed well-meaning organizations blame society, though the organizations emerge out of society itself. And government molds itself around the society, so that it can exist without too much inner turmoil, not confronting that which it is not committed enough to attempt to change. It becomes the mutual benefit of the conglomeration of all our misdirection. 'Society' is defined as the voluntary association of individuals for common ends. Often that 'common end' is to blame. Whether it is the small family unit, or the larger government of nations, blame can be the focus ...rather than seeking solutions.

If children are not to follow the ways of society, then what direction is provided for them? Children often possess only a very limited understanding of the significant roles they play. Their lives include family—-which they don't choose, and friends that they do choose. If the families choose to blame, then the children choose to escape.

One of the most common modes of escape is television. The other is friends. And the friends that they choose are often friends from similar families who have their own unique private sessions of blame. They share a common ground of inflicted blame. Together they often find comfort in viewing the other dysfunctional families often portrayed on television. And together, their own negative experiences and those of television, help socialize them. Once their own personal inner pain is added, they are thrust into the angry path ...to find their own way.

So society is made up of families we don't choose, and friends we feel we do choose, but not really. Friends become avenues of survival. And it provides an avenue for when we grow up and—-we can blame society too.

* * * * * * *

Somewhere along that misguided path, Mom had felt the need to see a therapist. Much time is spent talking about her childhood. It's safe because they aren't here ...Mom's own parents aren't here. But her children are here. They are in the next room.

It is too risky to talk about the husband-wife relationship. Each can't blame the other because it might make matters worse. But obviously Mom feels it can't get much worse. And she doesn't want her own anger to become too big of a factor.

Murray and I have no choice. We have to go to the sessions with mom. But we have to occupy ourselves in the next room. Murray sees there's a large selection of games to play with. But I'm more concerned with the games that are being played next door.

I pick up a book and sit next to the wall. I find that I can hear most of what the therapist and Mom are saying. I recall one particular session. It is particularly bothersome:

Mom: "I hit the dog with the broom. It really upsets Sweeney. He really loves that dog."

Therapist: "What do you think you can do to prevent yourself from hitting the dog with the broom?"

Mom: "I don't know."

Therapist: "Well, I can make a suggestion."

Mom: "What's that?"

Therapist: "Make sure that when you get angry, don't pick anything up."

Mom: "That won't work. I kick the dog too."

Therapist: "Why do you think you take your anger out on the dog?"

Mom: "Probably because it's Scottie's dog."

Therapist: "Oh, a case of transference."

Mom: "But Sweeney is the one that really loves the dog."

Therapist: "That's good insight. We're making good progress here."

Mom: "Not really. That's why I came to you. Insight has not helped me improve my anger. When Sweeney was just a baby, the dog was just a pup. I couldn't stand the dog right from the start. I tried to just ignore the dog, but I'm expected to do everything around the house. I tried to leave the dog alone, but I had to take it to the vet. It was suffering from malnutrition. I realized that if I didn't take care of that dog, no one would. My husband wasn't taking care of it. It was his dog, but I have to take care of everything in the house."

Therapist: "I hear you making reference to your house, not your 'home'. You don't really consider it a home, do you?"

Mom: "No, I feel it's an area I'm assigned to. I have to take care of everything, and keep everything clean. And all that dog hair makes me angry. I tried to not let it bother me. For three months I tried to stop caring about those things. For three months I didn't clean or vacuum."

Therapist: "And how did you feel during those three months?"

Mom: "The dog didn't bother me during that time."

Therapist: "So, you did arrive at a solution then. That tells me something."

Mom: "Yes, it told me something too. The dog didn't bother me because the house was so dirty, I couldn't find the dog. I couldn't find the children either."

So much for listening in on mom's therapy session. I look at the book I'm holding in my hand. It's by Dr. Seuss. Some people go to Doctors or therapists, but I have often turned to Dr. Seuss. I enjoy all his books. Dr. Seuss is certain to understand my plight.

Two children, way too young to be home alone, sit by a window. A window Dr. Seuss is about to open for us. Where is their mother? I see the similarity, yet at the same time, the difference. My mom is always there, at least in body.

These two books are my favorites. Even now, as an adult, I can recall the story. Yet, it may appear to have a slightly different slant …as I am no longer looking at it through the eyes of a child.

It all begins with an intrusion. The two children stand in silent amazement. Only their fish speaks. Rather fishy, right? Not really. The fish is their conscience, telling them all the things their mom wouldn't approve of. But as the children continue to look on in amazement, the *Cat in the Hat* somehow boldly states that——the tricks he will show them, their mom will not mind at all if he does them.

Then when the *'Cat'* introduces *'Thing One'* and *'Thing Two'*, the children shake hands. An agreement of sorts is made, with a certain degree of peace established about the whole thing.

Once again the *'conscience fish'* says the *'Things'* should not be there when their mother is not. But the children look on with simple amazement at the wrong things they are experiencing, until they see their mother returning home. Only then do they make a real effort to stop that irresponsible *'Cat'*.

But still looking for an out from the mess, they allow the *'Cat'* to take care of it. And they show joy at seeing that the problem is taken away. Then they return to the window to sit silently, as if nothing had happened.

All this encourages the *'Cat in the Hat'* to come back, when their mother is away for the day, of course. And before they can speak for themselves, he invites himself in. This time they say the things that the *'fish conscience'* would have said, but the *Cat's* answer is that they should try it sometime. The children take a stance and say 'No!', but each time a problem arises, they look to the *'Cat'* to fix it.

Each time they holler at what the *'Cat'* does wrong. Each time they witness the *'Cat'* making things worse. But each time they allow him to fix his own mess he continues to make.

The children say it's bad, but the *'Cat'* insists they should try it. Each time they are told that it isn't so bad. The first mention of dad follows. The reference is to how unsatisfied he'd be. And to avoid disappointing dad, they ask if the problem can be solved—-you know it can!! Undermining, underhanded, under way—-under his hat, the *'ABC Cats'* take the lead. And things get worse!

But the *'Cat in the Hat'* can fix it—-with *'Cat Z'*. He has something called *'Voom'*, that cleans up, fixes everything. We had let a little pink in. Then all we could see is pink. Soon we can't tell the difference between pink and red. We don't want to see red. We'd be no better than the ones who brought this all on in the first place.

The *'Cat'* is like society. Maybe I can blame the *'Cat in the Hat'*. But not really. I can see it more clearly now. Our spiritual life is like that. Without anyone to help keep us accountable, it can be like the 'Cat in the Hat' story. It would be better that we never let the 'Cat' in the house in the first place. And the more you let the 'Cat' fix the very problems he creates, the worse it gets.

The *'Voom'* took care of the mess, but you know what else it did? It all but guaranteed that the 'Cat' will be back. Do you know why? Because the 'Cat' was allowed to take care of the problem he had created.

Now, don't get me wrong. If someone causes a problem, it's often good to allow that someone to fix the problem they've caused. But not if *'they' are* the problem. And the *'Cat' is* the problem. He does things we know shouldn't be done. And he encourages us to keep it from our parents.

* * * * * * * *

Sweeney had thought he'd grown beyond these old feelings, but they are still able to drag him down, out of the best of moods. He refocuses. It is not this old hurt that he needs. He needs the new realization to lift him out of the doldrums. He will receive his blessing—-not from his dad, but from his Heavenly Father.

****

Sweeney is not the only one who has not fully developed a good parent-child relationship. Shannon had also experienced difficulty in this area. And at this moment—-discouragement, doubt, and deception join forces to attempt to defeat and destroy her.

Shannon recalls Sweeney's tears of confession. She feels sorry for Sweeney—-the way he burdened himself with guilt all those years. She can certainly relate to that feeling. But the words that return to her now, are only spoken through transferred emotions. Sweeney had said he respected the fact that she so deeply loved her dad—-something he felt he never really had with his own dad.

Shannon cries. Dad had every reason to doubt her love. Though he struggled at times with Mom, the love he knew was there ...is what always kept him motivated. Family meant everything to him.

As Shannon's tears fall, she grips Dad's hand, and cries aloud, "Though you may not recall a time I've told you this ...I love you, Dad!"

Try as she may to resist it, the worst of regrets consumes her. The fact is, she can only recall her lack of showing Dad that she loved him. She kneels down at his side, "Oh, God—-please don't let him die!"

* *** **** ***** **** *** *

Murray approaches slowly, seeing how much Sweeney is hurting.

Sweeney catches a glimpse of his brother, and speaks up first, "Impossible ...that's the best word describing Dad and me. Why do you think that is?"

Murray steps alongside his brother, "Maybe because you're like him in a lot of ways. But those are good ways. You are both the take-action type. And you both have a bold sort of confidence."

Sweeney wipes a tear away, "Do I look confident to you?"

Murray rests a hand on his brother's shoulder, "As soon as I got off the phone with Dad, Lorvin asked that I talk with you. He wants us to stay on. That's the sort of confidence we're talking about—-confidence in the faith."

****

As they get off the boat at mission headquarters, Sweeney assists transporting Shannon's Dad into the hospital. The Doctor requests only the nurses be present as he does a thorough checkup.

Shannon doesn't want to leave Dad's side, but she waits outside in the hallway.

Sweeney delays his departure, placing a hand on Shannon's shoulder, "My dad left us when I was fifteen. I tried to take care of mom and my brother after dad left. And I did a fairly good job of it, though he may have resented me for that. I envy the love you have for your dad."

There is no denying tears for Shannon. She swallows hard, unable to respond.

Sweeney doesn't expect a response. He forges on, "My dad is still critical of me. That's what makes it tough. When I was eighteen, my dad went in for heart surgery. Even though he had abandoned us, we still loved him. After his surgery, I stayed by his side. When he came to, he tore into me. The Doctor said dad was still groggy from the anesthesia, but he'd return to normal within the hour. I did not tell the Doctor that this was normal behavior for Dad."

Shannon continues to wipe her tears with the back of her hand. Sweeney puts one arm around her, and pats her on the shoulder, "Your dad is so blessed to have you here, —-you have what I have always dreamed of. You risked your life to save his life. My dad never seemed interested in any meaningful aspect of my life."

Maggie, one of the two nurses assisting the Doctor, happens to overhear the conversation in the hallway. Sweeney kisses Shannon on the top of the head before he departs, "Take care of yourself, kid."

The Doctor leaves the room. Maggie comes to the door, "It's okay to come back in now, Shannon."

Maggie is very sensitive and understanding. She does a lot of listening. She is not in it for gossip purposes, but for insight into the hearts of others.

Maggie may listen a lot, but when it's time to speak, she speaks, "Sometimes when we are feeling a lot of hurt, we try to help others—-which is a good thing—-but sometimes the advice is better served in helping ourselves."

Maggie places her forefinger under Shannon's chin, gently lifting it, "Are you having a difficult time sorting it all out?"

Shannon looks back through teary eyes, "It's so ...it's ...not what it seems. Dad never really ever acted distant from me—-he loved me. He showed it all the time. It was me who never showed it."

Maggie does what comes natural to her. She opens her arms. She does not speak at this time—-she just hugs Shannon. And when they are both tired of standing, she sits with her within the room.

Neither of them say anything for a long time, then Maggie prepares her for what lies ahead, "We are trying some new medicine in hopes to give some chance of survival. But the struggle may prove to be too much. Your Dad is in a coma-like state right now. No one has ever recovered from that advanced stage. This new medicine has hopes to change that. It is supposed to bring them out of that coma-like state ...but it is not expected to be a peaceful deliverance. It'll take great determination and a strong will to live. That almost insurmountable struggle that lies ahead ...well, I don't know if anyone can overcome that. But if he does make it through, it is at that time you can put all your regrets behind. It is then that Dad will need you. It is then that you will need to be there for him."

Shannon looks into Maggie's eyes, "When do they begin the medication?"

Maggie encloses her hands around Shannon's, "Hopefully, tomorrow. We don't have it here. We had to send for it as soon as we heard you were coming. We expect the plane may be arriving back tomorrow."

Shannon can't imagine the struggle that is ahead, "Has anyone survived as a result of this new medication?"

Maggie wishes she can give Shannon more hope, but she must be honest, "No, we've only tried it with one other person."

Shannon doesn't wait to ask, "So, what happened?"

Maggie doesn't mean to dishearten her, "We don't know yet. That other person is the old Chief. Early yesterday morning we gave him the medication. We had to move him to another building because his screams were so intense, he was scaring the other patients. But sadly, we have to take these desperate measures. It is believed that our only chance is with the hope that these violent seizures that the medication causes, will force him out of the comatose condition."

Shannon has to ask, "Aren't any of the rest of you afraid you are going to get it? Isn't it highly contagious?"

Maggie smiles, "We just recently received a vaccination for it. You'll be getting your dose within the hour."

Suddenly, Maggie is paged. She hurries out of the room, kissing Shannon quickly on the forehead before departing.

Shannon is left alone to dwell on everything she'd just been told. She wonders whether Maggie was called to the other building where the Chief is. She tries to blot out the thought of the torturous event he must be going through. She will be witnessing it herself, soon enough, with Dad. He will be getting the medication. She can't deal with those thoughts right now though ...so instead she resorts to prayer.

Shannon is interrupted once as they bring her dose of the vaccination. Then she continues to pray for Dad and the Chief.

Few people command such an immediate response, but one of them is Rebekkah. She had demanded to talk with Maggie. But once Maggie realizes she'd been called out of the room for a mere phone call—-and not an emergency—-she is certain to tell the person about it, "I was sitting in the room with Shannon when you called. I find that much more important at this time, than discussing the book with you."

Rebekkah realizes it as true, "You're right. I'm sorry. That's not really why I called anyway. I just found it easier to talk about the other first, then leading up to the more painful issues. I ran a cross-check on that bloodwork. Th-e the sic-k-k Ch-ief is real-ly Crazy Larry—-that prisoner that ...."

Rebekkah gets all choked up, and can't continue.

At this moment Maggie asks, "Is Cindy there? I'd like to talk with her."

Rebekkah quickly regains her assertiveness, "You know you can't tell Cindy about this—-it would tear her up inside. What if Stephen doesn't make it? Most likely he won't. Let's be honest ...you don't expect him to make it. So, do you still honestly think it would be good to tell Cindy that her husband is alive—-only to tell her the next day that he died?"

Maggie has enough assertiveness in her character to challenge what she thinks is proper, "To be honest with you, I think it unthinkable not to tell Cindy. If she doesn't know now, then she can't pray for her husband during a time when he needs everyone's prayers. And if you are thinking that Stephen will most likely die, and she should never know ...then you are creating a huge burden for Shannon."

Rebekkah insists, "I don't know—-I just know I can't tell Cindy, that's all. I don't want to burden anyone."

Maggie insists, "Well, then—-I'll call her. You can't just not tell her. Someone's got to tell her."

Maggie would perhaps understand more how Rebekkah feels if she knew that her husband actually has a son ...and *that* son is

Cindy's husband. Rebekkah fights to prevent those angry emotions from taking over again. Over fifty years ago she had received that startling letter. Then over a decade later she'd traveled to a maverick molecular biologist in England to verify it. And poor Ruth—-the fantasy that she'd created, pretending her son was her and Stephen's son—-poor Ruth never knew it truly was Stephen's son. Ruth went to her grave—-not knowing. And Rebekkah doesn't want her own son, nor anyone else to know either.

Would Maggie tell her own husband that it is his son that is about to die? Rebekkah will not give her that option. She hadn't told Ruth, and she isn't going to tell Maggie either.

Maggie had paused. She has one more point she wants to share, "And by the way, the plane that went to get the medication also dropped off the manuscript I've been working on for you. They shall be arriving in the States in a day or two. I just want you to know how difficult it has been for me all these years. At your pleading, I promised—-but I'm sorry I did. I believe it was wrong for me to promise. But I did learn something from it. I learned never to make a promise. And going over all these manuscripts has also been a burdensome task. Trying to keep them hidden to preserve the secret my husband doesn't know about you—-well, it is sneaky and deceitful. I can't imagine how you managed all these years to ...."

Maggie had said enough—-probably too much. She should have left that last part out. If Rebekkah is going to receive her words, she would have by now.

Perhaps Rebekkah has received Maggie's words, but is still a ways away from acting on them. It seems that is always the case with Rebekkah. She has spent a lifetime avoiding it—-but now, just this past year, she let Maggie know that she was preparing to tell him. But, she doesn't fault Maggie for not believing her. Rebekkah had begun writing a book entitled, *'So Loved....'*. She wanted to write a book to explain to her son how much she loves him. She knew how difficult it would be to tell him how much she loves him, since she spent most of his lifetime avoiding telling him so. But she felt the book would adequately explain why she felt she couldn't tell him, at first—-yet, how would he respond to her not telling him when she could? And then ...feeling she couldn't again.

Rebekkah had started by collecting some of his poems—-the collection entitled, *'So Loved ...'.* Then she worked a story around some of the poems. But instead of finishing the first book, she began writing a second book. Maggie's response at that time was to send Rebekkah a poem of her own, entitled, *'It's Never Too Late'.*

The second book was supposed to bridge the gap between her not being able to tell him, then when she could—-then not being able to again. This is the book she was about to complete ...having been a long time in coming.

Maggie recalls telling Rebekkah that she seemed to be writing more for herself—-that it appeared to be her own rationalizing and justification. And it appeared she would never tell him. It was taking so long to write, it appears she is using it as a stalling tactic.

Rebekkah had claimed it was because details were missing from the story, and she had politely asked for Maggie's help. But the story dragged on and on. She had decided that the last half of that second book would make a good third book. Maggie had said she was no longer curious whether and how Rebekkah would tell her son—-as long as she told him. This was taking ridiculously long, but nonetheless, Rebekkah had committed to the trilogy. She claimed she was eager to get it into print, but as Maggie sees it—-she is no more prepared to tell her son than she'd ever been. The truth is—-she's spending most of her time doing what she has been doing for a lifetime ...avoiding the truth, at least the telling portion of it. And she is asking yet another friend to help her write the final chapter of a story which she says she hopes she can play her part in—-helping to create a more pleasant ending for—-actually, for all.

******

Maggie will not be making any phone call. It is Shannon's place to talk with her mom ...if and when she decides to do so. If Shannon happens to believe the same as Rebekkah—-that they should wait, and only tell Cindy in the event that the medicine works—-then Maggie would do her best to try to convince Shannon that it's the wrong approach. But everything said and done, if Shannon still agrees with Rebekkah ...then Maggie will just try to respect that.

Maggie does not need to concern herself. As she enters the room, Shannon is on the phone, "I'm doing fine, Mom. How about you? You sound tired ...must be all that celebrating. By the way, happy birthday, Mom!"

Shannon had prayed. She's a bit more relaxed now ...actually, more than a bit. She seems like a totally different person. The prayer has not only brought her beyond tears, but to a conversation that actually appears rather lighthearted.

Shannon smiles as she listens to Mom's response over the phone, "Well, technically speaking, it is my birthday. But it's only a couple hours past midnight here. But don't worry about that. It's always so good to hear from you. I know you must be caught up in everything—-it's a wonder you remembered my birthday. But you are always sweet that way. I miss you so much, Shannon."

Maggie listens as Shannon replies, "I'm so sorry, Mom. I didn't mean to wake you. I never could get those time zones straight."

Mom laughs, "Don't apologize. I know you don't get much occasion to call. And you know I'm worried sick about you all the time. The best thing you could have done for me was to call. You don't know how good it is to hear from you. It always seems like forever to me, but I know you don't get a chance very often."

Shannon is eager to move on with the conversation, "Mom, I have to tell you ...I've had the most fantastic adventure here. God works wonderful miracles in the mission field—-sometimes way beyond our imaginations."

Shannon can't see her Mom smile. Everyone back home was aware of Rebekkah's surprise shipment. Mom imagines part of the reason Shannon hadn't called sooner was that she had received her surprise Arabian horse, and she had probably ridden it every day from dawn until dusk, thinking of nothing else. But Shannon is so sweet. She had remembered her Mom's birthday.

Mom misses her so much, "Yes, way beyond our imaginations. I imagine you'll be coming home soon. You will be back in time for your sister's wedding, won't you?"

Shannon is preparing to spring her surprise, "I planned on leaving for home last week, but something came up, and I've been rather busy ...but I'm doing my best. I hope you don't mind me bringing someone home with me."

Mom laughs again, "Oh, silly me ...for a second there, you had me. But you're talking about the horse, aren't you?"

Shannon draws out the suspense, "No—-that was a wonderful surprise, but this is an even bigger surprise."

Mom teases, "So, you met someone? The wedding bells will still be ringing in my ears from Leah's marriage ...and then you?"

Shannon knows she will win this game of teasing, "No, it's not my marriage I'm referring to ...it's yours."

Mom laughs, "That doesn't sound like you, Sweetie. I know Fernye has a knack for matchmaking, but don't tell me you are into it too."

There is a long pause. Shannon is beginning to get caught up in her tears again. And Mom is just caught in quiet reflection. She knows Shannon is just kidding, but she doesn't understand the sudden silence.

Mom asks, "Are you still there?"

Kidding aside, Shannon fights back her tears. "Yes, Mom, I'm still here."

It is so awkward and difficult to gauge emotions over the phone, but Mom tries, "Is it Leah's wedding that you're referring to? Are you worried that I'm going to try to take over her wedding ...and not give her any breathing space? Is that why you said my wedding ...because you know how I get? Well, I don't blame you ...I do sort of get carried away. I get all excited, and want to do this and that ...but you know how it is with me. You know that when you say my wedding ...you aren't talking about my wedding. You know I will never remarry. But I can still get excited about one of my children getting married. I guess you can tell that I am a bit tired ...rambling on like this, and not making much sense."

Shannon fights back the tears, "I didn't say your wedding, I said your marriage. You've made it clear to all of your children that you would never remarry. And that fact has made this occasion most beautiful."

Mom yawns, "I guess you may be a bit tired too ...being through so much lately. I imagine the mission field is a real challenge."

Shannon draws a deep breath," Mom, I don't know how to tell you this, but ......"

* * * * * * * *

Through many tears, Shannon manages to tell Mom all about it. And Maggie listens to the blessed sharing of this most joyous revelation, capped with prayer.

Neither Shannon nor Mom can figure how this all came to pass—they just stand ready to offer their thanks in prayer. Only two people really know the truth of what happened—-and they may not live to tell it.

At this point, what really matters is not knowing how it all happened, but knowing the One who not only knows exactly what happened, but also is the only One who has any control over what is about to happen.

Shannon and Mom pray together while on the phone. They pray to their One and only God. And before Cindy hangs up the phone, she tells Shannon she will catch a plane in the morning, so she can join her.

* * * * * *

Meanwhile, in the adjacent building, an intense struggle is going on—-not just for truth, but for mere existence. A lifetime of events and struggles flash within this tormented mind—-a mind once belonging to who most would refer to as—-Crazy Larry.

Now it is difficult to discern who that mind belongs to. Or who even cares. He counts four: Mom, Nanny, Maggie, and *this* Stephen. For the entire time he was 'Chief', their *caring* seemed only for their tradition, which benefited most of them to a degree. The *Chief* was just like a piece on a chessboard ...but, if they lost the main piece, it was not so disappointing. They would enjoy starting the game over.

But, the entire island is praying for the old Chief now. They don't consider it important who he really is—-he is the old Chief to them—-but, more importantly, they now view him as a person, and every life is valuable.

Shannon had heard Dad talk about Crazy Larry. Then had come the prison break and their disappearance. Next was the verification of them in the article about *'Make a Wish Foundation'*, placing them on the boat which had led to the report of their presumed death, later accepted as fact. But then, with recent confession by Murray and Sweeney, they were able to piece more of the story together. And yes, they now feel there's a chance that Old Chief and Crazy Larry are one and the same person.

Shannon is drawn away from Dad's room. Her Dad will really need her tomorrow. Meanwhile, there is a life that can really use her prayers now. And it will give her an idea what Dad will be going through tomorrow. She will endure the screams of terror. She will go to his side—-whether he is referred to as Old Chief, or as Crazy Larry. No matter who he is thought of as …she will pray for him.

****

Anyone could see the agonizing physical pain he is going through at this moment—-and anyone near could hear it too. No one should realistically expect anyone to endure this. But no one is here to really see or hear …except an occasional look-see by a doctor or attending nurse. In complete isolation, what could anyone really do anyway? All they can do is wait …and pray.

Though none of us can see the ordering of events, nor can we understand the real necessity of it …God sees.

In order to struggle back to sanity, Crazy Larry has to pass again through events in his life. They were torture enough the first time, but now are being repeated. Is he to order back a memory filled with disorder and confusion—-and attempt to gain back the sanity that most claim he never had?

Though most of us would imagine it preferable to erase those memories, it is necessary to recall those agonizing moments, to restore the memory and preserve the mind …or is that just a psychological conundrum? How nice it would be to be able to remember some of the nice things—-if there were any. The ordering of significant events, after all, is considered the foundation of our memory—-our sanity.

* * * * * * * * * *

Dreams, nightmares, and reality are all mixed together—-and have to be sorted out. As the mind orders up these events, as usual, the memory begins with childhood:

Other children call their caregivers *"Mom"* or *"Dad"*, but I think I'm special because I am the only one who has a *"Nanny"*.

I'm quite sure my Nanny loves me, but she also appears to love something else. You can tell just by the look in her eyes. Her hands are on cleaning or at times cooking, but she moves about in strange ways. A curious sort—-always trying to find something out. Of all the people in my life, she impresses me, and her ways are sure to create a great impact upon my young life ...and it begins my hiding around the house, always near to where she is.

I will not be left out of this game. I will find out what she finds out.

Soon, Nanny and I hear something I'm certain we are not meant to hear. Nanny gets caught listening and gets fired. I fear I'm going to get fired with her, but my hiding place is good, and I'm not about to let anyone in on it. Apparently, this family loves secrets and there is much they haven't let me in on.

I'm confused and concerned. I overhear something they obviously wish to keep secret. According to them, I do have a Mom like the other children. But they talk like my situation is different from that of the other children. From what I hear, my mom is supposedly diagnosed as having a rather severe case of retardation—-mentally handicapped, they say.

They say her name is Callula. The strange thing is that I know this person. I see her a couple times a year, during the holidays. I don't know why they don't let me know this is my Mom. Everyone else I know has moms who aren't kept secret.

I decide to talk with her during the Christmas gathering, while everyone else is busy talking.

She says I am her son ...she has overheard them talking about it. The way I figure it, they either think that she can't hear, or that she can't understand. I think it's ridiculous of them to think that way ...just because she is retarded. Sometimes it's difficult to tell who are the slow ones.

But I hear that's common for normal people too. So many times, parents talk in the next room and think their children can't hear. Or they talk in bed at night ...thinking those little ears are asleep, unable to hear in the quietness of the night.

I have a very difficult time dealing with all of this. I guess I made it difficult for them too, not having Nanny around to take care of me anymore. They'd probably initially hired her to help keep me out of trouble. I could've still managed that, if not for something they'd left lying around ...a number, Callula's telephone number. They must think children can't hear, or read.

The rest is simple. I call the number and ask for directions. I then take a bus.

The bus driver is very helpful also. I tell her I'm lost, and I'm looking for my Mom. She drops me off right in front of the mental institution.

Mom doesn't appear happy, at all. But when she sees me, she is happy. And I stay with her all day. She says it is the best day of her life.

It's soon night though, and I'm tired. I curl up at the bottom of her bed and fall asleep.

When they find me there, they are not happy. Mom is not happy that I have to go, but I promise her that I'll be back.

Though they make it difficult for me to keep that promise. They make some arrangements through some church people. I don't like my new home. I don't know much about foster care, but what I do know I don't like. I know I don't like all this shuffling around, and being away from Mom. And I know Mom doesn't like being away from me. I know it didn't go over too well the last time I visited Mom, so this time I decide to sneak her out to visit me. The key to it all is that I do it at night, and I always make sure I sneak her back by early morning.

I know Mom isn't happy at the mental institution, but I should have just stuck with my night-time unauthorized visits. I got away with it for a couple years ...until I began thinking she'd be happier at the foster home, and that they'd accept her there. That is my big mistake. I bring her back with me one night, and she falls asleep at the foot of my bed.

After that it's 'shuffling time' again. This time I'm moved to a group home. That's when the fearful things enter into my life. The man in the group home spends most evenings in front of his television. He always has it on his sports station, and he has it on real loud. He also drinks several cans of something, and belches really loud. The woman in the foster home does not appear the least bit interested in any of this. She puts earplugs in, and goes to bed early.

It's really loud ...but I like *'loud'*. It makes it easier to slip out at night. It's easy for a while anyway ...until this man begins to visit. He is certainly no stranger to me. This man is part of that group which spends time together, only during the holidays.

They say his visits are actually necessary to maintain funding for the home—-something to do with State regulations. I see State regulations somehow mean a regular beating. But that is nothing compared to the treatment one of the older girls in the home receives. She is no stranger either ...only the situation became stranger.

This Khaki Mae is only eleven, yet older than me. She's also been at the holiday gatherings. But she must've been kicked out just like I'd been.

Not long after that, I find out from Mom that the man who beat me is actually my father.

I am the only one who feels Mom is not crazy. She says my father is the sick one ...preferring to keep all his eggs in one basket. And he doesn't like anyone to be well. He prefers his eggs to be cracked ones. No one will believe Mom—-she is just cracked. And of course, being her son, I befall the same judgment.

Crazy Larry's entire body writhes in pain, going through a sequence of seizures, too long and too intense for life to endure—-at least medically speaking. Yet, locked inside are those agonizing memories.

Mom is considered insane—-and I am too, in believing her. But I am sane enough to know to never share with anyone the secret she tells me. I am best to just deal with the horrible fact that the man who was beating me and abusing the older girl at the group home, is my father. But during my last visit with Mom, I am told a much more disturbing fact ...about this older girl. She is my sister.

I am in total shock! I'm told that my sister does not know this secret. But knowing now that she is my sister, I soon become very angry. I hide, and actually watch what dad does to her during his abusive visits. He kisses her on the lips, and she seems to go into a sort of trance, as if separating herself from reality. I am convinced that she is not aware of what he does next, detaching herself from what is really happening. I want to run out from hiding and attack my dad, but I'm afraid.

I have to do something about it! After all, she is my sister! Yet, though I am *not* afraid of what he may do to me ....I am uncertain how it may affect her. She seems to be coping by escaping reality. What would happen if she was forced to acknowledge the horror?

Is this just an excuse? Why am I paralyzed with indecision? I know I'm going to end up hating myself if I can't stop this!

It gets worse, if that is at all possible. Subconsciously, she must be fighting that which she seems not to even acknowledge as happening, as she strikes out at what she must perceive as what the reason is, and the beginning of it all ...the kiss. She begins punching herself in the mouth. And blood is everywhere.

The next day her lips are all swollen. She is walking around as if nothing had happened, until suddenly she angrily throws a magazine across the room. I wonder what set that off ...so, I go pick up the magazine. It is *'Models'* magazine. I don't get it ...then I do. Though all the photographed models do *not* have the same color hair and eyes, and each have their unique facial and bone structure, it highlights what they all have in common ...their large luscious lips.

I never see the bloody lips again, though it appears she has done damage ...and they remain bigger, not the natural look for her. I see another change then. She now begins eating and eating ...and eating. I figure I know why she is eating so much—-and I begin to give her my food too.

I see that as she eats and eats—-she gets bigger and bigger. She just sits around and belches and performs other sundry gross functions.

Soon our dad, whom she didn't know of, no longer comes around. I am very thankful for that, and I am very thankful for her. I somehow feel her gross mannerisms are responsible for his not coming around anymore. And that means I am no longer beaten, and she no longer has to endure the horrific things done to her.

Crazy Larry's body stops shaking. Shannon wonders whether he is still alive. She is too frightened to get closer, but she must. He is sweating profusely and she checks his pulse. His heartbeat is racing. Suddenly, he grips the rails of the bed, his fingernails cutting into the bottom of his palm, causing it to bleed.

I really look up to her. She is the reason I no longer am visited by my dad for these senseless beatings—-sometimes nearly beaten senseless. I see her clever ways. Once he stops coming around, she stops eating so much. She only eats here and there. But she continues to keep the weight on. That is a mystery to me, until I happen upon her secret.

I see her sneak out of her bedroom one night—-and I follow. She goes to the basement. There is a room down there set up as a weight room. And that's where her secret is revealed to me. She doesn't see me. But I see as she peels off layer after layer of clothes—-and some stuffing that she'd duct-taped to herself. I see that she isn't big anymore—-or rather she is big in another way. She is now becoming very muscular.

She had turned her weight into muscle, but she still stuffs her clothes to make it look like she hadn't changed. It is a real art, and she is really good at it. If I hadn't seen it with my own eyes, I would have never known.

Then one night, she sees me. I promise I won't tell, but I don't think she likes me. She doesn't like anyone sharing in her secret—-and I think she still fears that man will come back.

At eighteen, my sister leaves the group home. With too many painful thoughts and memories ...I fear I'll never see her again. I hear she wants to become a nurse. There are many things I want to end up becoming, but as a few short years pass, I end up in a private mental institution ...with none other than my sister as the nurse. I discover that our father owns the facility, but I'm certain she never knew of this connection to the place ...nor his relationship to her. I begin to realize what Mom had said about my father keeping all his eggs in one basket. He's still successfully maintaining control, keeping us always edgy and choked with fear. It's sick the way he keeps us all within his wicked and watchful eye—-his basket of 'cracked' eggs.

She continues to wear her armor—-in fear that if she doesn't, he'll make himself known in the way he had in the past. She does a good job at making herself look big. But if you know her secret, like I do, you can tell by the muscles in her hands.

At the mental institution, I meet someone who I oddly trust from the very beginning. Her name is Maggie Major. And it is quite an experience knowing her. Previous to this, I've only trusted two people in my life—-Nanny and Mom.

Crazy Larry begins shaking the bed. This time his entire body doesn't shake—-just his upper torso and arms.

I am only trying to help the helpless young man. It seems all my sister's horrible memories are being taken out on the young man. She strips herself of her armor. Now dressed like one of those All-Star Wrestlers, she exhibits her quite unbelievable form ...from all those driven agonizing hours of workout.

She picks up the young man over her head, as if to say that no man will ever control her again. Then she slams him down, slams herself upon him, and pins him to the floor—-before leaping up with arms raised in victory.

It is scary! In an attempt to show that she will not be controlled, she is fully demonstrating that she still is. I fear for the young man's life. The inevitable is soon to happen. And the confrontation leads to ....the accident.

An attempt to save the young man's life—-costs my sister hers. And I land in prison, where I rightfully feel I belong. They also question me about the disappearance of someone by the name of 'Stephen'. That must be that young man's name ...but, I will never tell them how Maggie helped me help him. I just hope she was able to really help him. She is so wonderful ...if anyone could help him, she could.

Shannon cries and prays—-cries and prays. She prays he is not caught in past destructive memories. The mind is not merely a receptacle of past experiences. New ideas can also enter the mind. She prays that his mind will be renewed.

Suddenly, it gets real quiet. She wonders whether he's alive, as he lies there so deathly still. She immediately checks his heartbeat. It has slowed considerably ...and he is breathing normally. Shannon can't bear being away from Dad's side any longer. She kisses the old Chief on the forehead. She whispers, "God be with you." And she departs.

The thoughts do not depart from Crazy Larry though. He sequences through his past:

I recognize the connection with one of the psychiatrists at the prison. I had actually seen him one time before, at the mental institution, but the possibility of the connection scares me. Then there is another *'Stephen'* that comes into my life. What is it with these *Stephens*? Every time there is a *Stephen*, something happens. And sure enough it happens!

All the lights go out, except for the light of the fire. Everything is out-of-control. No one really knows what happens inside of a prison, except those who witness it—-and that truth is locked up inside a person, in fear the truth may escape.

The truth is, I feel no one cares what might happen to us. I feel it's up to us to find our own way out. But some of us are trapped within our rooms by the wall of flames.

I see another light, scanning about randomly, occasionally flashing against the ceiling. I suspect it is flashlights, as I hear Casey's voice down the hall, "Every man for himself! You gotta find your own way out!"

The flames are so lively one minute, I can't imagine how they are diminishing so quickly. Then I see that faint form. Someone has a fire extinguisher ...but that someone has nearly extinguished himself. The last flame being extinguished is the last glimmer of light. And that last light is barely enough to see that faint form fall to the floor.

I react! I have to save the person who had attempted to save me. I somehow feel it must be Stephen behind that bit of heroics.

Now I must save him.

It's pitch-black, but I gauge the distance from which the figure has fallen. I try to pick him up, but I'm not that strong ...I think it's this medication they have me on.

I need help, but I can't count on any of the guards. The flashlights are no longer in the area. Casey had taken charge, and the others had obviously followed him. He's not going to help a prisoner. He won't even help a co-worker. Casey will only help himself.

I holler out to Tennessee Trucker. I know he will help me. And he is stronger than anyone I know.

34

Trucker follows my voice, his strong arms gathering beneath my straining effort—-picking up our fallen hero with ease. I run into my room and grab my sheets—-I don't know why, but they come in handy. I recalled using sheets in the foster home to make ropes to climb out of the second story window. There is no second story here, but I grab the sheets anyway.

My eyes begin to adjust. It is an overcast night, but for one brief moment the clouds part, and the moon illuminates part of the fence. There is a gigantic hole in the fence. Within the lights of his vehicle, the perimeter guard is seen cautiously approaching on foot. I have to act before he reaches the hole in the fence. It is a very windy night. I wait until the right moment—-and I then release the sheets.

I run towards the sheets—-screaming. Trucker knows what to do. I had created a diversion. Every prisoner knows well what a diversion is. He breezes through the hole in the double fence—-the moon's light helping him avoid the razor wire strewn about.

The moon moves back behind the clouds. I don't see Trucker, I just see the guard standing in the light of his own vehicle. He raises his rifle, and aims at me. I don't think my screaming was such a good idea. I think I would have gotten shot by the perimeter guard if Trucker had not dropped what he was doing, or who he was carrying ...to grab the perimeter guard.

He squeezes him until he falls into a heap. Then Trucker does what he hasn't been able to do in years ...he gets behind the wheel of the truck.

Trucker drives to where he had dropped Stephen. Yes, by the lights of the vehicle I see that it is, in fact, Stephen—-no one else would have tried to save us. The lights of the vehicle now illuminate the area of the fence, so I can step through the hole, and avoid the razor wire.

I can never stand seeing anyone injured or in trouble, especially if it's life-threatening. I run to the guard's side. A pulse, still breathing,—-must have the wind squeezed out of him. It's a real relief that he is alive. I also relieve him of fifty dollars from his wallet. After all, there is another life that I must be concerned with—-that of Stephen.

When I get to the truck, Trucker reaches down within his tucked in shirt.

Trucker hands me a bag. I look inside. It's his playing cards! He has every one of his decks, his precious possessions, in that bag—-and he is giving them all to me!

I don't know what to think next. Trucker says he's going back.

I don't understand—-but I do. He's been locked up so long, he is afraid to face the outside world again. In a way, prison isn't much different than his trucking business. It's an escape—-one he's not ready to escape from. The very reason he took to trucking was to avoid confrontation—-to avoid interactions for the most part. And in the system—-that makes for a model prisoner. The ones who do the best in prison are the loners—-as long as they are left alone. And with Trucker's size and strength, everyone leaves him alone.

Clothed, and with three square meals—-Trucker has what he wants. The trucking business he'd previously worked for had become too confrontational. His peaceful job had become less than peaceful. Rumors circulated of illegal substances.

And that load fell upon Trucker.

Prison isn't so bad, for some—-it is the process of getting there that is bad. It's the confrontation—-the arrest—-the judgment—-the less than humane treatment. But now he is in prison, and he can be a loner again. And furthermore, he is respected and accepted by all the other prisoners. As I see it, it's a clear choice—-the prison, or the outside world?

The 'outside world' is too unstable—-he'll stay.

I'm so touched by Trucker giving me his prized possessions ...his playing cards. I want to give him something in return—-but what do I have to give?

I give Trucker a hug—-but am thankful he doesn't hug me in return. I don't want to end up like the guard. I really want to offer him something, but what do I have? "You can sleep in my room tonight. That is—-if you don't mind not having any sheets. There's still a blanket and bedspread for you."

* * * *** * *

I've only driven a few miles when there is a car blocking the road. I imagine they may be setting up roadblocks to try to stop me, but how could they have responded so quickly?

Then I see something I can relate to. Someone is kicking the car. It isn't a blockade. So, I stop.

A young man is going to take a friend to the midnight movie, but his car keeps stalling out. I tell him I will trade—-I'm good at fixing cars. He says he really likes trucks, and his friend will really be impressed if he picks her up in one. He points to the house he lives in—-and says I'm a real pal. If I get the car fixed, he says I can take it for a spin.

I get it fixed, and take it for a spin. I spin it all the way to -—Maine.

I try to blot out all the things I've done, but I can't. I was sent to prison for something that wasn't my doing—-I had tried to prevent it. I still feel guilty, but it wasn't really my fault. I should not have been sent to prison, but now that I'm out, I'm finding myself doing all the things I don't want to do—-my whole life I just wanted a chance to start over.

So much of my life I've been called crazy, that I just acted the role. I'm in this mess in the first place because of a long list of injustices—-and I'm beginning to hate myself. The only time that I actually ever felt any hope at all ...was just before I had gone to prison, having met Maggie. She made me feel special. I want to have her high set of standards. But those days are over. Now I'm turning out to be exactly what everyone expects me to be—-and I'm doing the very things I hate.

What is this torment of injustice? "If you can't beat them, join them"—-it's a terrible solution.

One wrongdoing leads to another. Now I'm a fugitive.

I took the money. I took a car, or traded a car—-which really was stealing. *'Make a Wish Foundation'* becomes my next lie, and I become a stowaway on an airplane. I really hope 'this Stephen' doesn't get airsickness.

Once we land on the island, I can barely walk. The plane ride was so long—-and in such a cramped area. Stephen is really sick. He had smoke inhalation from putting out the fire—-then I was so driven to escape, I stupidly stuck him in the trunk, and exposed him to more fumes. Then when the boat caught on fire, we jumped ship and he nearly drowned. Now I'm airsick—-and nauseous from all that refueling. I can't imagine what this is doing to Stephen.

When they go to greet the others before unloading the plane, I make my escape. I can't escape my guilt though. I should leave Stephen here and let them take care of him, but instead I steal a small boat and take Stephen with me. All I want to do is escape. I just want to get away—-from everyone.

But obviously I don't want to run from everyone. After all—-I have Stephen with me. If he survives, I can tell him how I saved his life. We drift for days—-upon days. I'm getting sick, but he's beginning to come to. I'm not fully aware of his sudden improved condition though—-until he stands up. I can't believe he has the strength to stand, but he does—-and he falls overboard.

The boat has life preservers. I don't know why so many of us refuse to put them on—-feeling it's okay to just have them in the boat. It's like strapping a helmet to the back of a motorcycle—-a lot of good that does.

I quickly grab the two life preservers. Instinctively, Stephen is flailing—-not swimming, but thrashing. I don't know if he can even swim, I just know he isn't doing too well at this time. I throw both life preservers at him. One of the preservers hooks one of his flailing arms, remarkably keeping his head above water. At least one thing has worked better than I expected.

I jump in after him—-have to get to him before his arm gets loose.

So much for preparing to tell him how I saved his life—-I'm almost killing him in the process. I took him from a fire and brought him to a fire. Twice fumigated him—-once in the car trunk and another time traveling *fugitive class* air travel. And now this makes twice that I almost drowned him.

By the time I reach him, his arm is almost out of the strap. I pull on it once from behind, then with amazing ease, I'm able to slip it over the other arm. I quickly clasp it in front. Okay, I reached him in time. He's safe and secure—-now to get my life preserver on.

I have a much more difficult time getting mine on.

I have a backpack on—-and I'm sure a life preserver isn't meant to go over a backpack. I'm so exhausted—-no energy to even worry. I have no idea where I really am. All I can see is water, water, and more water. I'm so tired.

Stephen already appears asleep. I put my arm around his neck to keep his head from dropping down. I want so much to sleep too—-and I do.

When I awaken, I feel so relaxed—-moving smoothly through the water with my arm still around Stephen.

I guess I'm rested enough to start worrying again. Where is my boat?

And I also hope the waters don't contain anything that might consider us part of the food-chain.

The scorching sunlight glimmers across the water, blinding my vision, so I close my eyes again. It is so relaxing. It feels like we're gliding slightly faster through the water than I'd anticipate from a simple drift. I let my mind drift once more, imagining how at times people had reported being saved by dolphins.

I let that thought drift for only a second or two, before I turn around and open my eyes gradually.

I see that it's not a dolphin, nor is it 'on porpoise'—-but it's not by accident either—-why are we drifting so quickly? Perhaps I'm hallucinating—-hunger, thirst, and exhaustion—-all playing a factor, along with this blinding light, and wishful thinking. I close my eyes again, this time opening them more slowly, allowing more time for my eyes to adjust.

I see a shadow. My vision is still blotchy from the intense sun refracting zillions of prisms of light from each surface droplet, extending out for—-forever, across the boundless waters. I focus hard. The faint shadow is—-my boat!

I turn my head back as far as I can. Suddenly, I see that it's not my boat anymore! It never really was my boat—-I had taken it, but now someone had taken it from me.

There are two boats—-the one I had considered mine and the other one. The other one ...what other one? Another boat has us in tow, by a rope or woven vine, tied to the back of our life preservers.

Such a rapid transition from such peacefulness and tranquility—-to such a state of panic. It's a tribal people—-the type the missionaries so freely greet with happy faces—-but this is a reverse greeting. I don't feel like I can express myself freely—-it feels like we're being held captive.

I guess I can be thankful they saved us—-but, saved us for what? The facial paint is rather intimidating, not to mention the clubs and spears.

When we near their island, the water is too shallow to bring us in tow, so they literally begin to carry us by the back of our life preservers—-one on each side of each of us. Then they lower us gently to the sand.

I try to shore up the proper emotion—-to try not to show fear. Having been in mental hospitals and prison, I have a broad perspective on what should be the thing to do in almost any situation—-I think.

In the prison, I tried not to act like I was intimidated. That wouldn't work here—-I am intimidated. In the mental hospital, if I showed fear—-everyone else may likewise react in fear. I don't want that! Fear and spear may go hand-in-hand ...or from hand to heart.

I have no clue. I have no idea what to do—-but whatever I do, I feel I should do it quickly ...in a slow kind of way—-not to make them defensive.

I begin to breathe deeply, groan, and grunt. I feel this is probably universal—-and they'll think I'm in distress. I take off my backpack, in hopes they'll think I am getting a gift for them, rather than think I'm retrieving a weapon. I had taken a huge zip-lock bag from the airplane. It has first aid items and a camera inside. I'd also placed the precious gifts I had received from Trucker in the bag. It isn't much, but it's all I have. Food would be nice, but I had pureed and spoon-fed Stephen our last.

I'll show them how the camera works,—-they'll be amazed. Don't aim it at them, I tell myself, it may startle, or anger them. But I can take Stephen's picture. And I can use the flash for effect.

He is stretched out on his back on the sand. I don't realize he's 'coming to' ...suddenly he sits up! I aim ...'flash', he falls back.

The tribal people look on. Do they think I injured him?

It's an instant-photo camera. And I wait for the picture to develop. Then I show it to them. But they don't seem amazed—-they seem confused. And I'm afraid what confusion may prompt them to do.

One of them begins searching through my backpack, while another has the zip-lock bag—-and spills a deck of cards across the sand. To this—-they jump back!

A King, Queen, and Jack are facing up. There is a Joker too.

Perhaps the playing cards look as tribal as the tribe themselves.

I pick up another deck of cards and begin shuffling them in an impressive manner—-though I doubt they are impressed—-by the look on their painted faces.

I don't know what to do next, so I do the only thing I can think of doing—-what Trucker would have done.

I ignore everything around me, and I play Solitaire.

It seems I can do nothing right. Perhaps Stephen and I are doomed.

Suddenly the earth shakes. The tribal people take notice now—-but not of me. I try to mimic the sound—-with my loudest vocal blast. I throw the cards high into the air, and let them float back to their place on the sand.

Now I have their attention! I begin to draw frantically in the sand. I draw the mountain, pointing at the mountain.

I quickly grab another deck of cards, holding them at the drawing of the mountain top while giving another vocal blast ...as I throw those cards into the air. They jump back! Suddenly I feel no fear. I'm in control again. And I have their undivided attention.

I pick up several of the face cards and run to the water's edge. With another vocal blast, I throw those cards in the water. Then I pick up one of the life preservers, with the vine rope still attached, and throw it in the water.

Now things are working right for me. As I pull on the vine rope, retrieving the life preserver—-to my delight I see there is a playing card caught within.

It is at this moment that I realize the similarity. Stephen's shirt is as bizarre looking as the designs on the playing cards.

I point to the playing card and I point to Stephen.

I hold the playing card in my hand, and the photo I had taken of Stephen with the camera. I quickly put the playing card behind Stephen's photograph.

I show them Stephen's photo and quickly gather together as many of the playing cards as I can, putting them in their box, and placing them on the sand at the foot of the mountain drawing—-with Stephen's photo on top.

I dig a hole at the top of my mountain drawing.

I get two Jacks and place them on each side of the deck, and walk the deck up the mountain with Stephen's photo on top. Then I place the deck and Stephen's photo in the hole I had dug at the top of my mountain drawing. I cover them up with the sand, having the two Jacks walk back down the mountain.

The tribal people suddenly leave. I'm relieved, but I wonder what they will do next. I am not looking forward to their return, nor the anticipation of not knowing when that will be.

I wonder why I had done what I had done. But for the moment, I'm thankful. In a panic situation, people do the most bizarre things—-and even more bizarre—-others often follow them.

The next day, the tribal people return. They have a small platform on poles. They pick up Stephen, and place him on the platform. Then they begin carrying him up the mountain.

I hadn't even understood what I was doing, but they understood. The loud blast had sent Stephen from the mountain—-out to sea. Or had Stephen run from the mountain? Whatever their beliefs, or their understanding of it, they are now returning him to the mountain—-to pacify the mountain.

I follow. I feel obliged to see what they are now going to do with Stephen—-after all, it is my doing. Whatever they are about to do, I'm responsible for it.

They carry him to the edge of a deep canyon. At its narrowest point, there's a plateau about fifty feet away—-on the other side of the canyon. Several other men of the tribe come from behind a large tree with what appears to be a ladder, with ropes made of vines attached. With very precise movement, they swing the ladder out, and touch it to the other side.

To my amazement, they pick up the pole platform and walk, with Stephen, across their constructed ladder to the plateau. For the first time, I see one of the tribal people smile, as I cautiously crawl across to join them.

At the far end of the plateau is a cave—-or tunnel through the rock. Light can be seen on the other side. They place Stephen in the hole, and I watch as two men carefully scoot back through the narrow tunnel. After a couple minutes, they return without Stephen.

They then escort me back to the ladder bridge, and allow me to drop down on all fours—-to crawl back across, while several of them continue to smile.

About fifty of the men stay on the plateau as the makeshift ladder bridge is removed. Nearly five times as many remain with me and proceed down the mountain.

My first thought is to begin gathering food for Stephen. I begin placing the food on the platform they had carried him up the mountain on.

Soon they catch on to what I'm doing. They smile—-and emerge with a staggering amount of food they had already gathered and prepared.

They carry the food up the mountain and to the plateau. The fifty men appear grateful for the food we had brought them. But more importantly, I watch them bring some food to the tunnel at the other end of the plateau.

Three days pass where they bring food to the tunnel—-then on the fourth day Stephen crawls from the tunnel. A couple of the men help him back through the tunnel. They want him to eat, but not eat with them. He has to stay in his proper place through the tunnel.

I am so happy to have seen Stephen, I get there early on the fifth day. Once again, I see him crawl from the tunnel—-and two men drag him back to where he belongs.

The sixth day, I do not see Stephen. I wonder if they'd been so frantic about him leaving the tunnel that they might have hurt him.

On the seventh day, Stephen does not crawl out—-he bolts out!

He gets past nearly a dozen men before they even have a chance to react, but then—-react they do!

I think I understand the motivation for each. The tribe feels that for the mountain to be satisfied, Stephen cannot escape. They want to return him back through the tunnel where they feel he belongs.

And of course, I cannot deny that this is mostly my doing. I don't know what I thought I was doing, but I somehow had brought them to believe this.

Of course, what I didn't tell them is perhaps the most fearful of all.

I didn't tell them what abilities the *Man in the Mountain* possesses. So, they've no real idea what they're up against. Perhaps he can leap that fifty feet from the plateau to the other side. After all, they believe he had escaped before—-they don't really know how, but they obviously fear what might happen if he escapes again.

Stephen, on the other hand, is motivated out of love. He has to get back to his family—-somehow!

The tribe responds as one. It seems they feel they have to stop Stephen before he reaches the end of the plateau. We'd just brought all of them the daily ration of prepared food, so some of the men have a much greater distance to go—-but that distance is quickly diminishing.

Stephen shows some rather unbelievable moves to get past the frontline of defense. It looks like a highlight film of the best of the NFL. He breaks one tackle after another—-as they unsuccessfully try to stop him.

As Stephen reaches the end of the plateau, he suddenly realizes that there's no way out. He looks up at me—-only fifty feet away, but across that dreaded canyon.

Impressed by his drive and determination, I throw up my arms to signal "touchdown".

The men standing with me also throw up their arms. I walk past the men, and give each of them 'high-fives'.

The men on the plateau begin forming two straight lines behind Stephen. I anticipate they're preparing how they're going to grab him—-to return him back through the tunnel. But to my surprise, they also throw up their arms. Like a Military Honor Guard, they are all lined up ...but they are smiling. These men appear to be standing in apparent appreciation of Stephen's grand effort.

Stephen turns around suddenly, and throws up his arms.

He walks down between the two lines of men, giving them all 'high-fives'. Then he turns back to me.

I will never forget the conversation that takes place next. It isn't really what Stephen says. It's more of what I tell myself. I feel terrible at this moment, as if I suddenly believe what my father had said—-or I'd imagined he said.

I very seldom had any individuals come into my life who were encouraging—-who made me feel good about myself, not until Maggie came along, and—-now, with Stephen.

Now, the only one who can come close to understanding me or caring about me—-is Stephen. I still believe he cares, but he doesn't understand my fears.

Stephen does attempt to understand, "Well ...that was certainly entertaining, wasn't it! Anyone on this island speak our language, Larry?"

At this point, I don't know if anyone speaks my language—-the language of fear. I'm afraid of myself—-my own failures. I don't want to be accountable for anything. I've been held accountable for something I hadn't done—-and had gone to prison.

Now, all I want to do is run away and hide. And I feel this island is as good a hiding place as any.

I feel accepted here in a strange sort of way. My whole life has been a strange sort of way. But no one here will make me face any of that. I only have to face Stephen's questions, "No, far as I know, no one speaks our language."

Stephen takes a deep breath, "Well, I guess it's up to you and me then. I hope you can do a lot better than me with the what, where, and how categories—-'what' are we doing here, 'where' is here, and 'how' in the world—-or 'where' in the world, and 'how' did we get here?"

I had long been proficient in evasive techniques, "You forgot the why question—-I believe that is probably the supreme question."

Stephen tries to avoid tension by attempting to be slightly more lighthearted, "You mean, why the reversal of roles? Why are you now free, and I appear to be the one held captive?"

I've been in so many therapy sessions throughout my life, I know just what to say, "Are any of us truly free? Those of us who think we are free, are often imprisoned within ourselves."

I have to step away at this time. I don't really believe in what I was about to say next—-so I don't say it. How am I going to tell him that I saved his life twice, maybe three times—-when it was I who had put his life on the line? And I should expect him to be grateful—-for what?

Stephen probably doesn't consider this being saved.

All he would care about at this time would be his family—-they are his life. I'm not giving him life, I'm helping take it away. But I still can't be sure what would happen if I tell these tribal people that he is not really the 'Man in the Mountain'. I can't deal with all this guilt.

I'm afraid to make any more decisions, to take any more chances.

I decide not to chance letting Stephen see me again.

I will get rid of these clothes—-and clothe myself with the island. I want to blend in with them. I will paint up my face, and rub the earth into every pore of my body. And I will become—-as the earth. I will become the people—-the people of the island.

I try to keep myself hidden. Then something very strange happens. Our island is invaded by Komodo dragons.

I think they blame me. Stephen is believed to be the 'Man in the Mountain', but they seem to think somehow that I must be the *'Man of the Sea'*. And they seem prepared to return me there—-like they did Stephen to the mountain. Like they returned Stephen to the mountain to appease it—-they are likewise prepared to return me to the sea—-so the Komodos will stop coming.

I don't particularly like that plan, so I come up with my own plan. I begin herding all the Komodos—-to the canyon.

I amaze them with the cigarette lighter that I'd taken from the zip-lock bag. The entire tribe jumps back as I quickly produce fire. Then with huge fire sticks, I herd the Komodos. The tribesmen chant together, "Vea Viliami".

At that point, they make me their Chief. And one chief thing I make sure is always done—-the *'Man in the Mountain'* has to eat. And his guardians on the plateau have to report back to me—-whether the 'Man in the Mountain' has eaten, and whether he is well or not.

I feel I'm responsible for Stephen being here, and I'm going to continue to be responsible. I'm going to keep him alive. He may wonder, for what? But, I will keep him alive.

There is something to be said for being alive.

Suddenly, Larry tosses and turns. This is the last phase of his struggle. Whether he lives or dies will be determined by his will to live. And deep inside Larry, he still can be called upon to be responsible, even though he doesn't understand much about what is going on.

Stephen had taken ill about the same time Larry had taken ill. With him not being well, he is uncertain whether anyone else will take care of Stephen. Larry can't assume anyone else will—-it's his responsibility. He has to be sure to check on him. If Stephen isn't okay, it is no one's fault but his own.

****

Cindy's emotions are now all over the map—-from unbelief to grief—-from hysteria to prayer—-from relief, thanks, and eager anticipation—-to uncomfortable feelings of old. The feelings of old begin to dominate—-with fear of rejection. The lack of love, and the constant conflict spur on overall general bad feelings.

Cindy has to rid herself of the negative thinking. The best thing to do is to visit Fernye again, before she leaves for Indonesia to join her husband. Fernye is the most positive person she knows.

The walled community makes life so much simpler. Fernye lives just next door.

Out of respect, she calls first. But something isn't right. Fernye doesn't sound like Fernye.

Cindy hurries next door. She is greeted by both Fernye and Rebekkah. Cindy feels slightly hurt that Rebekkah knows more about all this than she does. But she realizes what a great asset Rebekkah is—-with her ability to get things done.

Rebekkah has already arranged Cindy's flight. She'll be leaving for Indonesia in a couple hours. Rebekkah also believes it is best not to tell the children at this time, "Let's see if Stephen makes it through first."

Cindy knows well how tempting it is to be swayed into adopting Rebekkah's opinions, but she is surprised that Fernye agrees. How is she going to explain leaving the country without the children knowing why. Fernye doesn't look well—-and she doesn't seem like her good old self—-she just looks old.

Fernye is the oldest person presently, though she has never seemed that old to Cindy—-not until this very moment. Fernye's positive attitude and uplifting character seems to be absent today. But she insists she'll be okay—-she just wants to rest.

Rebekkah always seems to excuse herself first ...to take care of last minute arrangements. Cindy goes back to her place to gather her luggage for the trip. What did Fernye think Cindy would tell the children? Was she to tell them that she is flying out to see Shannon, since she misses her so much? She would want the children to be open and honest with her—-so why tell only part of the truth?

She should be feeling good about this. There is hope she'd be getting her husband back. But she isn't feeling that way. She isn't feeling like she is gaining—-she feels like she is losing it. She feels absolutely miserable—-and she feels miserable because she feels miserable about feeling miserable.

Cindy feels Fernye can get all the rest she wants—-later. She'll give Fernye one more hug before she leaves. She knows Fernye won't mind one last pleasant interruption.

Cindy panics. Fernye is on the floor. And she barely has a pulse.

Cindy scoops Fernye up, cradling her in her arms. She knows she can get to the hospital quicker than an ambulance. She nearly sprints, carrying Fernye. Hurrying to the van, she gently leans to put her in the seat, fastening the seatbelt. She has to get to the hospital right away.

Pulling right over the curb to the emergency entrance gets the immediate attention of a couple nearby nurses. They attempt to assist as Cindy lifts Fernye out of the van, twisting around to lay her on the gurney they had quickly provided.

They are ready to wheel Fernye in, when Cindy collapses.

The hospital personnel bring Fernye back to life, but they say Cindy has now temporarily messed up hers. Her life will have to drastically change in the oncoming weeks, and they put Cindy in traction. She is not to move her back. And it may be weeks before she can.

Fernye comes to Cindy's hospital room, and positions a chair beside her bed, "You know how much I love you! You are the best Granddaughter in the whole world." She lowers her head to kiss Cindy's hand. She never does lift her head. Fernye dies there.

****

Rebekkah not only recommends that Cindy not tell the children about Dad, but now she says it is probably best that Shannon not be told about Fernye. She says it'll probably be too much pressure on Shannon at this time. Cindy feels this is too much pressure on herself, but she'll follow Rebekkah's lead.

Cindy knows that Shannon will have to be told something. She will be expecting Mom to arrive soon. But Cindy is in no shape to arrive anywhere soon. She'll let Rebekkah call and explain that she is in the hospital, but will be okay—-and Shannon is not to worry about her.

****

Meanwhile, Shannon sits quietly in Dad's new room. He'd just been moved to this other building—-so his screams won't disturb other patients. Soon he will be given that terrible medication.

Shannon knows that it is best she put aside those horrible images—-the intense struggle he has to go through. The terrible medication is also a wonderful medication. It is intended to save his life—-if it works. The Doctor is honest about it. No one has ever lived once reaching this advanced stage of the illness. This new medication doesn't bring much hope of survival, but they have to try something—-or there'll be *no* chance.

As the medication is administered, they all encourage Shannon, and pray with her. But then Shannon surprises them all, "I'd like to be alone with him while he goes through this."

Maggie feels the need to speak up, "You know, the Doctor advises against it. We've discussed with you how it will be absolute horror, watching him go through it. You shouldn't do this to yourself. It's too much to expect anyone to bear. Besides, you can always help him later if he gets through this. That's when he will really need you. At this stage, he won't really know you are even here."

Shannon insists, "I'll know that I'm here!" She doesn't tell them she had snuck in while the old Chief was fighting from the brink of death. All she wants them to know is, "It's my right to stay. Once Mom gets here, she can join me. Maybe he will be able to feel her presence."

They respect Shannon's right to stay ...but they privately decide to take turns outside the room, in case she changes her mind and needs them. Meanwhile, they all pray—-that not being something they merely take turns at.

Shannon recalls the Doctor saying that each struggle will have its own unique horror. Many factors play into the will to live. It is a combination of the past, present, and future.

The past has a lot to do with the person's proven ability to cope—-to rise above. The person's present condition also has a lot to do with it. Each day we can discount our past successes and throw no light on the future—-by our mere frame of mind. But that's the scary part. In this coma-like state there is no registered mind at all. And attempting to get the mind back is one of the biggest risks of all—-trying to bring the mind back to where it was before it had slipped away.

They all wonder what Shannon's frame of mind is at this time? Obviously, she is holding on with great hope.

They evidently have some hope also ...after all, that's why they are trying this violent drug. But, most of their hope is in somehow learning something through this experimentation. The chance of survival is very slim, but without trying it ...they feel there is no chance. It is still a difficult decision to make, allowing a person to go through this much pain and agony. Yet, they all agree that Stephen would unquestionably elect to do this if there was any chance he could be reunited with his family.

They are also in full agreement in the belief that it is not solely up to the person's will to live. There is *God's will* also ...and there is prayer.

They all know Stephen's past, present, and future concerning God. If Stephen dies, he will be with God ...that they are certain of. What they are not certain of is his present striving ...fighting to be reunited with 'Komodoville' may not be a strong motivation. How can he strive towards family when he can't even know they are there in the room with him, or are about to be reunited?

For Shannon, this is a much more difficult issue, not entirely convinced that it will make much difference even if he can know she is in the room.

Yes, it will make a difference. She has to convince herself that it will. She knows it will! She has to know it will. Just because she has never opened up to him, doesn't mean she doesn't know her Dad. In spite of her previous unwillingness to accept his love, he always continued to love her. That was true then—-and that is true now. She can't let doubt rule this moment. She is certain he loved her ...and if he ever makes it through this, she'll be there to tell him she loves him too.

"Oh, God, please give me a chance to tell him!"

****

She knows that soon Dad will be going through the unimaginable. She prays that it will not be as intense as it was with the Chief. Or maybe he will not have to go through it at all. But if that means death, then that is not her hope.

Shannon wonders if her prayer is a selfish one. Would Dad prefer to pass on—-to be joined with his Heavenly Father? And if that was his desire, would it be fair for her to pray against that?

Some would pray that he'd have no pain, and to rapidly recover. Others may say that they would pray for life, if it could be without pain, but if the pain proves to be too great, they'd pray for peaceful passage. But that's not the way Dad would look at it. He'd never question what God decides, but as for himself, he'd laugh and remark that he wouldn't go *this far* to merely give up.

Shannon thinks about all this. She can do nothing, if she does not pray the desires of her heart. She also will accept *God's will* either way—-but she will pray for Dad to live, even if it means he will have to go through seemingly unbearable pain.

After all, the worst pain imaginable is the heart wrenching pain of emotional unrest. She at least wants to be able to tell him that she loves him.

And Mom's flight will be arriving shortly. She won't be going through this alone. Mom will be by her side, sharing Dad's burden.

****

Dad begins to toss and turn. Shannon knows it's about to begin. She has to prepare herself—-for a nightmare of the worst kind. She thinks back to the writing assignment she had helped her youngest brother with. The assignment was to be about something that could be the worst imagined ...but she would never want to imagine this.

She remembers Samuel didn't much like the subject either. So they had changed the subject to pleasant dreams. They had talked about riding Arabian horses down sandy beaches.

Shannon had lived out that dream. She had ridden her Arabian horse on the island's sandy beaches. But she had found a truer love. True love is when we give up our dreams for what we truly believe in—-and she believes in Dad.

Only Dad can sort all this out at this point. Well, not really! Dad would be the first to admit it is not just his struggle. And Shannon also believes God can sort it all out.

* ** *** **** ***** ****** ******* ****** ***** **** *** ** *

As reality clashes with what may be imagined real, the collective ideas and thoughts that had become to be known as 'Stephen', begin to fall into place:

In Stephen's world, everything that was, ceases.

But if it ceases to be, then why the presence of the question? The lights had gone out, and it is so dark. When you are in complete darkness, you search for answers. But you find little comfort.

Everything is at a standstill. There is a big pause.

Nothing has direction. Doubt riddles any thought, or purpose.

There is no thought—-there is nothing.

How can there be no thought, yet still be this determination that everything is in darkness? To understand darkness, one has to have at one time been exposed to light. Conversely, to understand light, does one have to be exposed to darkness?

Sad as it may seem to be, suffering often is the chosen path towards appreciation of light—-of life.

In life, there is no escape to nothingness ...nor is there any need. But what most don't understand, neither is there an escape to nothingness in death. Death is a process, riddled with confusion, and denying the light. Death is not a single moment, nor an end in itself. It is a direction.

I know there will be light ahead. Light is a direction also. It is the path I have chosen. A path is a visible direction. Unlike darkness, it is not possible to follow unless it is made visible. It is a path of the heart—-which Jesus makes visible. And we have to enter that path before we pass on. That path provides for us a rebirth.

I feel like I'm falling deeper and deeper—-or am I traveling back to my own conceived beginning?

It feels like I am surrounded by water. It is so dark, yet strangely comfortable. This first comfort was in not knowing, birthed with innocence—-yet filled with busy excitement, poised and ready to be known. I still feel secure in returning to this first comfort, as the joy of knowing doesn't quite match this first comfort.

As I proceed, there are many comforts that draw me near. I hate to admit it, but some of these comforts are even false comforts. Yet, as the first comfort was in not knowing, a new comfort speaks anew in knowing.

It is in knowing—-that which reaches deep inside—-yet birthed from without, which defines this rebirth.

I no longer have the fear and doubt. They are emptied out of me, and I feel this rebirth. As they say, if we are born once, we die twice. But if we are born twice, we die once—-and live twice. The second 'twice', whether of death or life ...is eternal.

This is the most vivid of all. This was my purpose before all became darkness. I was trying to communicate to them about the Light.

They are mad. It's about Casey. They'd seen him leave the building. They know how long he'll be gone. Casey is very predictable. Predictability can be comforting, but it can also be tormenting. It's a brief moment of comfort now, for a time, until he returns.

At this moment they confront me. They know that I see what they see.

Max is first to confront, "How would you feel if you were told you were going to die tonight?"

I am not actually afraid of the prisoners. This is not a threat. I can see the desperation in their eyes, and in the nature of their question ...though I don't fully understand the motivation behind it.

Crazy Larry takes over, "I don't really fear death. But I know it can be scary to most people. And just because I don't fear it, doesn't mean I don't mind Casey telling us all the time that we're going to die—-telling us that death is in our food, in the medication we get, in the mattresses we sleep on ..."

Max adds, "It's not only that; Casey also tells us we are going to die and go to hell, to be tormented forever. He says there is no escape from it because we've already been sentenced. It's because of who we are—-convicted felons."

I look into each of their individual hurts and into their angry eyes. I do not show them anger in return. My eyes soften with compassion, yet speak boldly, "That's not true! Those who pass judgment are most in danger of it. We must all decide whether we believe what God says ...but, we are never to pretend to know, or judge how God will deal with each individual at a particular time in their life."

I know that these prisoners may never again approach this depth of seeking. I have to keep on talking, before I lose their attention, "I know that it is hard to imagine a place more tormenting than this one, but the truth is that there is a place. And those who flirt with the ideas of evil intent and attempt to befriend it, have no idea that evil has no friends, only pawns and prisoners."

I realize that I may not be talking on their level of understanding. I still have their attention with words like 'torment' and 'hell', but I need to focus more on the simple truth. "Before many of you came here, you likely were led down a path you had no idea where it was leading to. You were shown outright, or perhaps got lost and came upon it. But God shows us a path that leads to the place of no pain and no suffering. This place which has been prepared for us is called Heaven."

Stephen looks at this diverse group, and is uncertain whether they are comprehending this ...nevertheless, he continues, "And we have a guided tour down that path, so we don't get lost; or mistakenly take a wrong turn, leading down the wrong path. God wants there to be no mistake who our guide is ...we must follow Jesus!"

Max interrupts, "We are supposed to be guided by a baby?"

Crazy Larry laughs, "Jesus grew up just like we did. He didn't stay a baby!"

Max doesn't like the insinuation that he's stupid. He doesn't like to be laughed at. But he doesn't know what to say.

His best friend Harry speaks, "No, he didn't stay a baby, but he died ...just like Casey says we are going to. Is that how we follow Jesus? He died, we are going to die ...are we going to follow him into death?"

The group surrounding me does not look like a close-knit group. The only thing they have in common is their hurt and their anger.

A random observer may think they are like a street gang, ready to close in on me. But I know this is not the case. Past their hard exterior, I see a very scared and concerned group.

I find myself getting more intense, "No, we follow Jesus into life! Jesus did not just die. He walked out of death into life ...something we need to do."

They all begin to feed on each other's wild ideas. They are polite enough to take turns, but they are not really listening to one another. They pick up on key words and phrases, then blurt out whatever crosses their minds:

"I know that! But it was the angel. The angel rolled the stone to the grave away. The angel gave Jesus life."

"Yeah, the angel heard about it ...and with those huge wings, a couple flaps and they can travel halfway across the universe. It happened when my mom died. A huge storm came up. I was scared, but the wind was actually coming from the flapping of the angels' wings. The angel brought my mom back to life, but wanted to keep her safe from my dad, so the angel turned my mom into a Canadian goose, so she would be protected."

I know they are taking each other on a wild goose chase, creating more and more wild ideas. No matter whether it's magic, wizardry, or reincarnation ...it's all wrong.

I have to stop this nonsense, but before I can, another prisoner blurts out, "That's right, that's what it means to be born again. My brother died, and he came back as my dog. That's what they mean when they say a dog is man's best friend. Actually, I knew it was my brother ...I could tell by his eyes."

I can't stand it anymore! I interrupt loudly, but not rudely, "Now listen here!"

They return the look, penetrating and challenging.

Yet surprisingly they do listen as I challenge them in return with my strong conviction, "Prison is a humbling experience. I'm assuming most of you don't like prison. Well, you better be thankful for your time here. The advantage you have here is that you don't have the distractions of the world."

I find myself becoming confrontational, and as soon as I say it, I regret it, "But you are also allowing your mental illnesses to distract you. Things are *not* always what they appear to be."

Crazy Larry speaks up, "It's not just our mental illness, it's people like him." Larry points out the window. Casey is returning. It is dark outside. Only the path is lit. Casey cuts across the grass. "Your co-worker is evil!"

I feel their frustration, "You're talking about hell and evil. I know you have fears, but how can I tell you the way out ...if the minute I say one thing, you all take over and make up ten or more wild stories. Even the stories that you try to tell that have some truth, may have enough untruth to bring about conflict. That's why you have to stick with the Bible, and precisely what it says."

I should've stopped there, but I also know Casey will be coming back soon, and I've limited time. As usual, I get too excited about these rare moments to share, "Most of the Christians in our country have been given some wrong information, in some form or another. Most of the wrong information is not as significant as all the right information we have ...yet, often the less significant becomes more a part of our belief system. What is rather more important ...is that we believe Jesus gave His life for us."

I want to mention how disturbing I find it that a belief system can be based upon thinking a dog is a brother, or a mom being transformed into a goose. Humor is on my mind, how they are barking up the wrong tree ...and not focusing on the one Jesus died on. And that thinking a mom can turn into a Canadian goose ...is going on a wild goose chase. But, they are way too serious ...and no subject is more serious than this one. I restrain myself from adding humor.

"It is not that important if we understand that the fruit Adam and Eve ate was not an apple; and that the wise men were not at the manger scene. It's important who Jesus is, and what He did for us ...not so much troubling ourselves that Joseph, Mary, and Jesus were not white."

Reggie gets excited, "I knew Jesus was black!"

Crazy Larry corrects once again, "No, Jesus was not black or white. He was somewhere in-between. He was Jewish."

I don't want to lose my point, "There's much we don't know. Don't focus on the part we don't know about ...stick to the parts that are talked about over and over. If you don't understand something then ask someone who you feel does know. Like when they talk about being born again. We are born again in the sense of seeing things in a new light. Each of you, when you were born, were precious and innocent. You still are precious, but you may feel you are no longer innocent, because you've been sentenced to come here. I can't honestly tell you that your judgment from your crime will be served with an apology. But I can tell you that life here on earth is not an end-all ...you will be able to spend eternity in a much better place than what you've found here. Accept the path Jesus has made clear for us. Be born again! Be born with no hatred, be born with no anger, be born with no bitterness ...and accept Jesus, accept His forgiveness, accept His sacrifice."

The group suddenly gets quiet. I wonder to what degree they understand what I'd said. They look at each other.

Max looks at Tennessee Trucker, "I don't want to hear all this! Casey just entered the building. He usually goes to the bathroom for seven minutes, then we're back to the same kind of ridicule and degrading attitude that has driven us down our whole lives. We all know that Trucker could take care of Casey. Or all of us together could take care of him, but we all know what would come of that. They would put us all into lockdown, not worry whether we get fed, and force us to urinate on our floor."

Reggie adds, "Some of us would probably end up in the 'hole' and we'd be treated even worse than we're treated here. We don't want to go through that. We want you to take care of it. We don't want to hear about this lowly Jesus. We want you to notify the proper people to get rid of Casey!"

I realize I haven't gotten through to them, but I'm not through trying. "We live in the United States, and you'd at least think we would be united enough to be able to rid ourselves of all injustices. But each night I pray for a small little nation across the ocean ...the nation of Israel. I have a heart for what all of you are saying, but that little nation has been through more persecution than any other people. They are God's people. God's people are not just Christians ...we Christians become God's people. Israel always has been. They were looking for God to rescue them from all their torment, so God sent His Son. I won't pretend to know all the reasons why the various people rejected Jesus, but I'd guess that some of the reasons were similar to some of the reasons why each of you may be rejecting what I've been saying."

Stephen tells himself that he shouldn't have said they may be rejecting what he is saying ...where is the positive thinking? He tries a different approach, "You want me to get rid of your torment ...just like the people of Israel wanted God to get rid of theirs. You don't want me to suggest that you tolerate Casey, as a concession to not make it worse for yourselves. And even more, how would you feel if I were to recommend that you pray for Casey? The Bible says that we should bless them that curse you, and pray for them that despitefully use you."

I suddenly feel I've really lost them with that.

Trucker begins to talk. He seldom ever talks, unless it's before he does something. "You mean that Jesus is God's Son?"

I was so into explaining, I failed to even acknowledge Trucker's question. It was as if I were speaking to myself, for myself. I was forgetting who I was speaking to, and the purpose for it.

I speak as if I'm on the campaign trail, speaking for my benefit, instead of God's purpose, "Just like you are tired of Casey's rule, I can see why the people of Israel were tired of the Roman rule during the time of Jesus. When they were told a Savior had been born, it may have generated both excitement and disbelief. Most of them believed somewhat in their history. They clung onto the wonderful stories of how they were taken out of the bondage of Egypt through Moses, God's chosen instrument of deliverance. But as we soon read on, they were not satisfied nor content. Do you know why? Because they hadn't been delivered inside. That's the deliverance God provides us ...that Jesus taught."

Trucker repeats, "You mean that Jesus is really God's Son?"

Max adds, "And Mary is the mother of Jesus, so does that make Mary and God, wife and husband?"

Crazy Larry is always poised to correct, "No, Joseph and Mary were husband and wife."

Reggie adds, "Wasn't God's mom's name Mary too? Isn't that why we pray to her?"

Crazy Larry corrects, "No, Jesus didn't ask us to pray to his mom or Himself, but to the Father."

Reggie concludes, "Oh, so we are to pray to Joseph?"

Suddenly, it gets quiet. Trucker looks angry and speaks angrier yet, "Stop it! You're confusing me! You're all adding so much. We are mentally ill. If we want to know anything, we have to shut up, and listen. So stop adding things and stop talking away like we can't read the Bible for ourselves."

I messed up so much with my attempt to witness. Trucker appeared to be the one who got their attention. It is not only those whom we label as the mentally ill who can get it all messed up ...we all can.

The Bible is 'truth'. If we imagine beyond the truth, then what do we expect other than something beyond true——which is by definition, untrue.

Yes, I was the main one who learned something today. I need to stay simple and central to the point. God's Word, the Bible, is available in many languages ...but, mostly to those who speak English, and especially available in the United States. Shouldn't the Bible be our focus? And that reminds me of what I've been back and forth contemplating for some time now. The story, *'The Essence'*, has to go. I'll take care of it when I get home.

It will just cause more wild confusion.

Amongst the confusion, the question returns. How did I get to this point in the first place?

Let's go back to the beginning.

Suddenly, it is as if someone releases the pause button.

"In the beginning, God created the heaven and the earth. And the earth was without form, and void; and darkness was upon the face of the deep. And the Spirit of God moved upon the face of the waters. And God said, 'Let here be light: and there was light.'"

Yes, thank God for the Light!

I am on the path Jesus has illuminated for me.

I just don't know what part of the journey I am presently on. That sudden light I am traveling towards—-is it the eternal light of Jesus, or is it the light of Jesus reflected in my wife and children's eyes?

The darkness—-it is back at the prison. I had extinguished the flame, but must have been overcome by those fumes. Then the light—-the blinding light of the salty water about to engulf me. Every pore of my body goes from being saturated to being parched as I vomit upon burning sands.

Suddenly the earth shakes. Unintelligible voices of panic fill the air. Swallowed up in the confusion, unknowingly, groups of people now begin to respond. Has the earth divided as a result of the earthquake? No, they once again come together—-having had long ago been divided. They are confounded. They don't understand. They will follow their own crazy ideas. They will choose their own, so called, enlightened ones. Yet I choose to live on with the truth that I know—-the truth that I pray others will know.

I live on, year after year, my wife and children growing older as I grow old—-but I am far from touching the light of their eyes. Without them I find little meaning in life. I pray to God—-oh, how I had neglected to pray to God. But now, I pray unceasingly. I even pray for all the crazy Larrys out there, and the so-called enlightened ones. After all, they are grossly misled ...and merely ignorant of the truth. Only by the grace of God, go I.

I pray to God ...and sing praises to Him.

But no more! Something has ceased my singing.

I've fallen into darkness—-not eternal darkness, but I've lost the light of my wife and children's eyes. I know the light has not forsaken me though. It will never leave me. It is a promise I cling to.

The shift between light and darkness is not a welcome change. Now, back in darkness, I long for the return of the light. The moments without light do not provide comfort. I long for the light to return.

Suddenly, I see the two paths clearly. I am drawn towards both directions, but I stand motionless. I am not certain how to choose, nor whether it will be mine to choose.

One choice is towards eternal light. The destination is pleasant ...with no pain, no suffering, and no tears or crying. I feel no pain going in this direction.

The other path is not easy. Absorbed within the intense light of the path to eternal life, it is impossible to even see the other light. But I know it's there. The light that has been placed within me shines brightly from within my heart. It's been placed within me by the light of eternal life. It defines my faith, hope, and love ...knowing what is there, even though I can't see it.

I can feel that sense of need ...a need greater than my own.

The smiles are not as they once were. I cannot see the light of their eyes, but I know that light is there. They are far away and it is dark, but faith allows me to walk through darkness, knowing the light that exists.

The eternal light is permitting me to return ...to go back, with the promise that the path of eternal light is my final destination path ...and I look forward to one day traveling it. But for now, I shall return to help comfort the tears, the hurts, and the confusion.

I hesitate! The smiles are perhaps ...no longer smiles? But they have their Mom—-to comfort them—-and to help them smile. She will certainly point them to the joy, to the joy 'Giver', the joy of God's love, through His Son Jesus.

Yes, they have a Mom who will do it all ...but she shouldn't have to!! She shouldn't have to do it all by herself! I joined together with her ...and I am her partner. I haven't always acted like one, but I love her, and I know without a doubt that she loves me.

As her partner, I can feel the pain. A certain pain rests within her that is inconsolable. And I know she hurts as much as I do. I must return back to her side.

Yes, I can now see the light of her eyes—-the children's too ...oh, so much more potential light. I love them all ...oh, so very much. And the children miss their Dad too. I will fight through the pain.

The suffering, no matter how intense it proves to be ...will be worth it, to get back to them.

Shannon watches as Dad fights on. It brings horrible chills down her spine. It's like a crime being committed, so terrifying that one can barely stand to witness it.

It doesn't seem fair. Yes, it could be perceived as just another in a long list of horrible daily injustices. A simple summation would reason that this is common for a world in sin.

She feels the panic of the world, all wrapped up in her Dad's shrieks of terror. Yet, though sin surrounds us, it does not have to reside within us. She is thankful for all the prayers. Dad's struggle thus far has not been as intense as old Chief's. But, for Shannon, it is much worse. After all, it is her Dad—-and the pain of watching him suffer is near unbearable.

XXXIV.

Maggie enters the room where Shannon is sitting with Dad, "Shannon, Rebekkah just called to say your Mom will not be able to make it. She'll be okay, but she's in the hospital right now. She injured her back to the point where the Doctors want her to be bedridden for a while. And it's probably best no one comes to the island right now. If your Dad makes it through, they'll want to keep him quarantined until they can run some more tests. And we're running low on the medicine to combat this disease. It might be a couple weeks before we can get more in."

****

Rebekkah hadn't mentioned anything about Fernye's passing. But the mention of the words, Dad and Shannon, left Josiah and Samuel staring at Rebekkah as they'd coincidentally entered the room at that very moment.

As soon as she'd hung up the phone, Rebekkah had departed. Cindy feels lousy. The feeling goes way beyond her back pain, to where it really hurts. Josiah and Samuel stand silently for the moment. They are looking to her for an explanation. They don't even know quite what to ask, but Cindy is certain she has to say something. She is not going to openly hide the truth.

Cindy tries to explain it, but it's difficult. Even knowing the truth, it's difficult for her to still comprehend that Stephen is still alive.

She knows she has to share it with them. So as difficult as it is, she tells them that their Dad is very sick, and the chances are against him pulling through.

Cindy is relieved that Josiah and Samuel make it easy on her. Though why would she think otherwise? All this stress is adding

81

more unnecessary stress. Josiah and Samuel understand the need for the quarantine. Besides, as much as they'd want to be by Shannon's side to support her at this time, they feel they should be at Mom's side to help her ...and also comfort her in her time of mourning at Fernye's passing. They will support Shannon and Dad with their prayers.

Cindy has the strength to beg for more of their understanding. She is still struggling with full disclosure. She asks them not to tell Leah about all this, rationalizing that if their Dad doesn't make it through and survive, she doesn't want to sour Leah's wedding plans. And if he *does* make it through, he can just surprise Leah and be honored by escorting her up the aisle.

Josiah and Samuel are so overwhelmed by the news, they don't know how to react. Josiah feels he never really knew Dad. He was so young when Dad disappeared. And Samuel had never even met Dad. They both loved Dad on video, but that was different. Now their hope is that they soon meet him face-to-face. It is what they want, yet it will be awkward, after all these years. They can't imagine what Mom is going through right now.

****

It is Leah's last evening at the abstinence conference in Grand Rapids. Several churches in the area are participating. They send two buses—-one for the girls and one for the boys. They are of high school age, or single adults. The entire theme is to stress honor and respect in relation to relationships inside and outside of marriage. But the central point is that certain things are only proper within the marriage relationship. The precious emotions of each young person needs to be acknowledged, but they also need to learn that they need not be controlled by emotions alone, but by abstaining from the things that lead the emotions into actions.

Leah understands all of this. But she doesn't understand the inconsistency she feels exists at the conference. She also doesn't understand why she seems to be the only one who feels this way. Why are they holding a dance for the final evening of the abstinence conference? Nothing wrong with common dance ...but 'grinding'?

Stan leads Leah to the dance floor, "Loosen up a little. Why are you so tense? This is just a prelude to our wedding night."

Leah doesn't much like this. The whole focus of the abstinence conference seems to be lost, as far as she is concerned. She looks about her. The look in everyone's eyes scares her. She looks into Stan's eyes, "We aren't having dancing at our wedding."

Stan's eyes are different from the others. His eyes are soft and loving, "I know, but it feels good to dream."

****

At their wedding, Leah dances with Stan. She had conceded to having alcohol and dancing. Contemporary Christian music plays loudly, and at the sound of a bell each young man breaks from his partner and switches to the nearest young lady for his new partner.

Leah recognizes her new partner. It is John Elefante, "I am supposed to give you a message, Leah."

John twirls Leah. The music blasts, "This is what love is ...this is what love is."

The bell rings again. A new partner steps in ...Dad? Leah feels really awkward. She is no longer thinking of Stan. She no longer desires that kind of relationship. She is so happy to have her Dad back, she isn't even interested in being married to Stan. But it's too late. This is her wedding. Pastor Tom had already pronounced them husband and wife.

Leah sits up in bed. It was just a dream.

But it was not just a dream. It was odd and rather frightening. Where did that all come from?

She looks around her. She is thankful the other girls are all asleep on their cots. It would be rather embarrassing the way she'd leaped up in bed. Leah still wonders about the strange dream. She feels no ambivalence about marrying Stan. She loves Stan more than she can imagine. And she is very relaxed about the idea of marrying him.

Leah tries to imagine what, if anything, this dream could mean. Sometimes a dream seems to be a product of our fears, sometimes a dream allows us to realize something, and sometimes a dream doesn't seem to have any meaning other than to confuse.

Leah allows this moment, while everyone else is asleep, for quiet reflection and prayer.

At such a pivotal point in her life, she realizes a thing about love. There are many kinds of love. And no one on earth would love her more than Mom ...or more than Dad had, for that matter. That kind of love is sacrificial. But what is most significantly relevant is that many loved ones are all praying for her ...praying to the One who knows all about sacrificial love. And Leah has always trusted their love and guidance ...and she trusts the One who sent His Son to sacrificially provide the only true way for us.

This love is a simple, yet deep love. All that is necessary is to accept it ...and this defines faith. And with the kind of love faith provides, Leah and Stan will hold hands in mutual love and faith as they proceed up the aisle to get married.

Leah relaxes back to sleep.

****

Leah will be returning from the conference in time for a funeral she has not been told about yet. Cindy has chosen not to tell her about Fernye until she returns.

Leah will be returning today. Today is still young ...it is 3:00 a.m., and Cindy has been unable to sleep. She cannot relax. She is in quite a bit of physical pain, but that is not why.

Cindy cannot relax with the idea of Stephen returning. It's been so long since Stephen had disappeared. And it seems so distant now, it doesn't seem possible that he'd be entering their lives again.

Her thoughts race ahead of her. First she has to plan the funeral for Fernye. That will be difficult—-though her Dad will help. He always makes things easier, but the difficult thing will be the sorting out of her emotions. Oh, does she ever miss Fernye!

But does she miss Stephen too? It frightens her—-the fact that the question even comes up in the first place.

But she can't beat herself up because thoughts enter in with her many mixed-up emotions. Often emotions return right back to where they were ...when the last encounter was. And there were so many encounters ...so many confrontations. Those life events weren't any one person's fault, but the guilt still lingers. It's like that in war too ...with the husband missing in action. The very nature of war can tear a family apart by the mere fact that the family is no longer one complete unit. Stresses enter the lives because of that intrusion upon your dreams ...and things often don't go well at home. Then when he is classified as missing in action, you worry because you love him ...you grieve, you attempt to cope, and eventually you may even accept the fact that he is not alive—-and he is never returning home. You have to cope with that! You have to make life comfortable—-at least do the best you can. And often that best is not the best, but it has become comfortable. To survive through the seemingly inconsolable grief you feel, you disassociate yourself from much of life ...and the only way you can cope is through maintaining that disassociation—-even concerning your husband. It's not that way for the strong ...but all are not strong.

Cindy tries to remember what Fernye had told her—-something about, when in doubt, let love take the lead. But presently, love is *not* leading—-fear is leading the way.

****

For Crazy Larry, the struggle is of an entirely different nature. All of the significant events of his life had flashed through his mind. Now he is resting in darkness.

It is really dark. When people are deprived of light, they strive to maintain sanity. They struggle for hope, for purpose.

The path Crazy Larry is on—-is not a path of light. It is not a path of hope.

There is no light on this path. And the only hope is to go back and find the light. But there is no knowledge of it—-no striving towards something that there is no knowledge of. You can't go towards something if you don't know it's there. Unless, of course, someone else guides you.

They continue to pray for guidance. But Shannon prays for—-neither the Chief, nor for Crazy Larry. She prays for neither by that association. She prays for ...not so much who he is, but who he could become. And she prays for her Dad.

The only thing that Crazy Larry strives for is to save Stephen. He sees the light—-the light of Stephen's eyes. And he goes towards that light. He has to save Stephen.

What he doesn't know is that ...the task is already done.

But he doesn't have to know that. God knows. And it is truly He who does the saving ...He who provides the light. That is often not clear to many of us, but it needs to be clear.

****

Stephen's direction is clear. While on the island, he will keep his mind spiritually and mentally sharp. He will recite aloud the descriptions of our Lord.

The Lord, God, who heals, sanctifies, and provides—-our Creator, our all-sufficient, Lord, and Maker—-our loving Shepherd, who sets the standard through peace and righteousness -—the Almighty, all-knowing, ever-present, immutable God. The song of praise rings out in Stephen's head:

El Elyon, El Shaddai,

Jehovah-jireh, Adonai,

Elohim, Jehovah-shammah. El Roi, Jehovah-raah,

Jehovah-saboath-tsidkenu-nissi-shalom,

Loving Lord, thank you ...Jesus, prepare for me a home.

****

Prepare a home for Crazy Larry? There is little doubt that if Crazy Larry survives, he will leave the island a new man. This island,

Missionary Island, as most call it, shares the knowledge that lights the path ...leading to God's eternal home.

Rebekkah, on the other hand, is trying desperately to find the earthly home—-and family, that would tie together that very complex story that few would be even interested in. But Rebekkah had been at this so long, she doesn't know how not to do it.

Rebekkah gets a call back from the lab. They've made a strange discovery. Two separate tests she'd asked them to run hadn't come up with any conclusive results, other than verifying their own identification. But there was a match from another sample they had on file—-this being the far-reaching benefits of computer technology.

Rebekkah is upset that she had not thought of this before. That old Catholic Church in Old Town, Maine—-she had been there. She'd been so close, but had come up empty-handed. Why hadn't she thought of it before? Catholic churches keep some of the best records—-and they never throw them away.

In this particular church in Old Town, a young priest invited all those who were good at cleaning. But sometimes asking for help, you don't really know what help you'll get. And the old records were mistakenly discarded. Oh well, so much for the forefathers of record-keeping! But the old priest, in turn, gave the name of an elderly nun who loved children, keeping her own records and praying for each of them.

Rebekkah is not feeling well the day before Fernye's funeral. She'd tried to track down the nun, but was none the wiser. Then finally, she receives word that the nun is vacationing in Israel, participating in a tour with an old friend, Ray Vander Laan.

Rebekkah passes the information along to another friend who will get in touch with the nun. Rebekkah has gathered all the information from the computer file and has everything pieced together, except this one last detail about Crazy Larry. Perhaps the nun can fill her in.

Rebekkah tells her friend, "I need that information. I'm going to get him, even if it's the death of me."

And it nearly is! Rebekkah has a mild heart attack.

Then it hits her again—-not another attack, but the continued reminder that what she is doing, what she has been doing all along, what she's been doing for a lifetime—-is all wrong. But she has continually failed to stop herself. Maybe this attack will stop her. She wonders if this is a big enough wake-up call? No, not really! She just needs a little more time. Then she will stop—-it all!

Rebekkah is told by her physician that she should come in for a check-up, right away—-but she says she needs at least another week and a half. "Ten days ...I'll come in for a check-up in ten days."

Meanwhile, she'll put together a video of her 'will'—-just in case.

****

Crazy Larry obviously has a strong will to live. Ultimately, the final say is not whether others pray for him to live ...or not. It will soon become obvious whether God wants him to live for some reason or not. The entire island already knows that God wants us to come to Him with our concerns, so they are very clear on their course ...and they continue in prayer.

On Missionary Island, life isn't always easy or pleasant, but everyone there shares in knowledge of what they believe are the two main purposes in life: To come to the acceptance of God, through Jesus, and then to share that personal commitment as a testimony, giving the message of salvation to others.

It's certainly not too difficult for Larry to see his world as condemned, waiting to face eventual judgment. And that makes it even easier to accept the salvation message. Larry has spent his entire life being condemned, culminating in the judgment by the gavel that sent him to prison. He had faced judgment ...it had not been rightly considered whether he was innocent or not -—he was doing time. He knows how it would feel if the judgment would be lifted and he'd never have to go to prison again.

Crazy Larry not only knows how he'd feel if someone took up his case and saved him from having to do any prison time ever again, he also understands very well how he needs saving from the judgment the world will eventually face.

The message of salvation is received by Larry the second day after he comes out of his coma-like state. It is clear that Larry was even more open to the message with Maggie presenting it.

There is much rejoicing throughout the island, yet Shannon is not ready to rejoice. She does not blame Larry for what had happened to Dad. She prays a prayer of thanks to God for Larry's recovery—-and also for his acceptance of Jesus as his Savior, God's righteousness for our sins. But she cannot rejoice. She has high expectations. Since Dad got his medicine two days after Larry had received his—-Dad should be pulling out of it any time now.

This is a critical time for Shannon. Will Dad pull out of it? She certainly isn't going to leave the room to join the celebrated success of old Chief, Larry—-there is plenty of time to celebrate later. Right now, she wants to be there for ...Dad. If he should recover, she wants to be there the very moment he pulls out of it.

Shannon's intentions do not gauge her level of exhaustion. When the body wears down, if we don't take care of it, it takes care of itself. But compared to what Dad is going through, she feels she can at least be able to stay awake. Surely she can endure that!

She is wrong! She collapses in her chair. Sleep will no longer be denied its privilege. It wins over her desire to stay awake. Yet her internal struggle spurs on many dreams—-dreams filled with fear.

Shannon has no idea what may be going through Dad's head. Likewise, she cannot sense what is about to go through her own mind either. While awake, we should be able to direct our thoughts and decide which ones to lay claim to. But while asleep, our honest struggles often reveal themselves in one form or another. There is no attempt to hide, yet there is no clear commitment to represent the truth either. Consequently, it may not make any sense at all.

It's obvious that Shannon is filled with much fear. And whatever preoccupies her waking hours, is now also dominating her dreams. Covering the past, present, and future—-fear is multidimensional. Much of the past fear originated when Dad disappeared, carrying on through those many weeks—-to the day the belief of his boating death was revealed. The present fear possesses the most driving force, directing itself away from destination hope. The hope that Dad will survive is combated by the fear of the possibility that he might not.

What about the future? If her greatest fear gets swallowed up within her greatest hope, then hope received, should dispel all fear, right? No, it is not that easy. The future contains its own set of fears. The potential weighs heavy with fears linking to the past and present. That makes the future the most complex of all. And it involves the fear of rejection.

Shannon's dream carries her to the past. It had been a large gathering for her birthday. She had eaten too much cake and was in the bathroom, near her parent's bedroom. Dad voices his concern to Mom, "I wish Shannon would just call me, Dad. I hear the way she says Josiah Stephen. I see the way she pinches his cheeks and kisses him. If he's so much like me, Josiah Stephen, then how come the bigger version of him is so unhuggable?"

Then Shannon's dream carries her to her favorite short story, the book Dad had given her: *The Princess and the Poppy*. She and Dad suddenly become the story, as they run down a hillside of delicate orange flowers. It is not the flowers they gather up. They gather each other up in each other's arms.

The past only gives her an overwhelming feeling of regret. But there shall be no future fears. There is no fear of rejection. She had rejected Dad, but she would never have to fear being rejected by him. Dad loves her. And if there be fear of what possible love she may have in return, she can simply dispel that fear by showing her love.

But fear makes its final bid. Up until this point, she has never shown Dad that she truly loves him. What if he really needs that love—-to help him pull through? What if he really needs to know someone is there, to give him hope? What if he is in danger?

Shannon dreams that she falls asleep by Dad's side. She could have asked someone, anyone, to relieve her. Any number of people would've gladly sat by her Dad's side, to help monitor him ...if she would have only asked! But she hadn't asked. And now she hadn't endured. She had fallen asleep.

She has let Dad down, when he needed her the most! He is in danger!

Shannon snaps out of her sleep—-screaming!

She has to get a grip ...that was just a dream. But, this isn't! Crazy Larry has a large straight edge razor at Dad's throat!

Crazy Larry puts the blade down, having finished his last stroke in completing the shave. He hadn't quite finished, but he is finished for now, having been startled by having startled Shannon.

Larry explains, "I thought he'd probably look more like your Dad if he had a clean shave."

Shannon notices that Larry is also cleanly shaven. She also notices Maggie. When Maggie found out that Chief was actually

Crazy Larry, she didn't know how to act. Crazy Larry had been responsible for saving the life of the man whom she in turn married. Obviously, she knew Larry better than anyone else, but she now realizes how much of a mistake it is to risk the trust that others may not share.

Maggie spares both Shannon and Larry of any further awkward introductions or explanations, "Sorry, Shannon ...I should have waited until you woke up. I just wanted to surprise you with seeing your Dad the way he used to look. Actually, it seems like that's what helped Larry pull out of it. I had just finished shaving him, and slapped on some aftershave. I don't know if the slapping helped or not, but Larry said he was aware of the overwhelming smell of aftershave. Why don't you try it, Shannon? It can't hurt to try. We can't just sit here and stare at him all day. We've got to try something!"

Larry apologizes, "I'm sorry, Shannon. I should have let Maggie or you shave him. I didn't mean to scare you. I've done so much damage, I just wanted to do something to help—-but I guess I didn't."

Shannon picks up the aftershave, "It's not your fault. You were just trying to help. I want to thank you. Actually, he does look much better now."

Shannon gently slaps the aftershave on Dad's cheeks, then steps back in anticipation. Several long minutes go by, and to her dismay, nothing happens—-the greatest of hopes, dashed. A tear runs down her cheek, then she half-laughs, "Dad never did like aftershave."

Overcome with emotion, she cries, "I know what you do like." She grabs him by the cheeks, "You are so cute!" She kisses him, then whispers in his ear, "I love you, Poppy."

Her vision floods with tears. She doesn't immediately see what Maggie and Larry see ...but she feels it! With her cheek resting against his, her tears streaking both their faces, she isn't sure whether she imagines it or not, but Dad's head seems to turn slightly. Then she feels it—-a kiss on her cheek.

Shannon wipes her tears enough to see what Maggie and Larry are already seeing. Dad's eyes are open, a tear moving down his face—-swallowed up in a wonderful smile.

XXXV.

Fernye had prepared her own message that she wanted the preacher to read when she died. This moment had come. It is rather easy to read:

"A funeral is not really about the one who appears to be the center of attention—-that is already a done deal. A funeral is really about all those left living. What are the living going to do with their lives? Okay, so some of you got kind of close to me. Of course, you'll be hurting right now. And I know most of you ...you'll do a fine job supporting each other. I have attended so many funerals in my life where there is more concern over how much an imposition into their own life the death has made ...than how really devastating it may be to the one who is truly grieving. I once saw a little girl lose both her parents. Would you believe there was more talk about how difficult it was going to be on the rest of the family, instead of considering what the poor little girl must be going through? Make sure to pause—-give them time to reflect on this one."

The preacher waits until the few chuckles pass throughout the large attending crowd, then he continues: "The only way we can truly look at life is through death. Much of our lives are otherwise rather meaningless and insignificant. We fill our lives up with things that don't really matter. There are few moments in life that we actually get real. The moments in life that I consider significant are moments we have to face grave sickness and disaster, most all moments in the mission field, births, weddings, and funerals. Since this is my funeral, consideration should be taken to honor my requests."

Yes, for those who know Fernye, this sounds like her style, "I only have two requests. Actually, I only have one. I should say I only have two expectations at my funeral. The first thing I expect is that people will cry. I don't have to request it ...I already know the ones who truly love me. And I am thankful that there are many of you. The second thing I expect is a request I have. I expect the truth to be told. Not the truth about me ...I don't want one single thing mentioned about me. Where I'm going, it's not about me. It's the truth about Jesus that I want to be told at my funeral. And afterwards, I want it to be told over and over. Then if you still want to talk about something, talk about the most wonderful things in life. Talk about births, and rebirths. And talk about weddings."

****

Leah looks beautiful in her full-length white wedding gown. An old man approaches. He is dressed in the old colonial-style attire ...the type you'd expect some of the early statesmen to wear. He even has that presidential hair-do, with the white curls—-like a scroll or old important document draped over his head. And he has a small pair of spectacles, resting halfway down his nose.

The old man approaches Leah and the groom. He takes off the spectacles and rests them on Stan's nose, "Here, I don't want to make a spectacle of myself." The old man takes the scroll off his head, and places it on Stan's head. The old man suddenly doesn't look so old.

It's the father and bride dance. Leah had not been in favor of dancing, but Stan had convinced her otherwise. The only time in her entire life she had ever enjoyed dancing, was in her Daddy's arms—-that moment, preserved on video, when she was only an infant. That memory served as a source of peace and comfort throughout the years.

And it provides that same comfort now, as Dad begins to sing, *"This is what love is ...oh, this is what love is."*

He can't sing very well, but it is a comforting voice—-the voice she has always loved. As he sings, he begins to dance with an imaginary partner, one hand up, and the other delicately to the side. Slowly, Leah steps forward. She times it perfectly, stepping within the place of the imaginary partner, gently clasping Dad's hand. This is a delightful dance.

Dad is choked with tears. He continues to dance, but cannot finish singing the song. The song must finish itself.

Before the song finishes, Stan cuts back in.

Leah smiles, "Who are you?"

Stan laughs. He is used to Leah's kidding. He holds Leah at arm's length and smiles, "I know I haven't properly introduced myself. That will have to wait until after the reception."

Leah screams, "I want my Dad!!"

Josiah leaps out of bed and hurries to her side, "It's okay Leah ...it's okay! We're getting our Dad back ...he's really coming home! That is not just a dream ...he's really coming home!"

Leah reassures Josiah that she'll be okay—-as he reassures Samuel and Mom, who stand at the door as he is about to return to bed.

Leah hugs her pillow and closes her eyes. Upon returning home from the conference, she'd been told that Dad is alive. It is so difficult to sort out all the emotions concerning that. But what she does not quite understand is why she had a dream about Dad the night before, not knowing anything about him being alive.

What is this inner conflict between Dad, and being married to Stan? Dad will certainly be in favor of her and Stan getting married, so what is it? Why the confusing dreams?

Maybe she just has to reconcile it. She is yet to see Dad ...that's what the problem is. Once she's reunited with him, everything will be okay ...and she will have the faith to move on with Stan.

XXXVI.

They've already set sail—-to bring Shannon and her Dad back home. She wants the reunion to be a happy one. She doesn't want to get in the way of it nor have anyone bothered over her. But she'll attempt to call Murray and Sweeney just one more time. Rebekkah is scheduled to leave within the hour, but she wants to make this phone call first—-before she leaves.

****

Meanwhile, though recovering at home, Cindy is still bedridden. She's exhausted, but being confined to bed doesn't prevent her from talking with her husband for the first time in seventeen years. Though much of the conversation they are having over the phone is not conversation ...it is filled with crying.

Between the crying, they do manage to tell each other how much they miss each other ...and love each other. Then they resort to crying again ...not audible cries, just where neither can talk.

This same pattern repeats itself over the first hour. Then the explanations begin. One of the things explained is that Fernye had passed away. Stephen is not shocked by that news. Fernye had lived way beyond everyone's expectations. Shannon is the one that takes the news hard. Mom and she were the ones who were really close to Grandma.

The news that Stephen takes hard ...is about his Mom. Shannon is glad she was not the one passing that news on. Cindy sheds many more tears, telling about how his Mom's health began failing not that long after his disappearance ...and how she just became weaker and weaker. This rips at Stephen's heart. He wraps his arms around Shannon. They cry together. They will be able to grieve together, and get much of the grieving aside by the time they are to arrive home. Then it can be solely a joyous reunion ...a celebration.

Shannon and Dad are in each other's arms much of the trip back to the United States. They are scheduled to arrive in the state of Washington in a couple days.

****

Rebekkah also has a trip—-that she can't refuse. She isn't looking forward to the trip, but it's one she must take. It's not the hospital visit on her mind. Her final destination will most likely come first. She's only nervous about how her last moments here on earth will play out. Four people she trusts will carry out her plans. They just have to!

But maybe she should have one more. Yes, she will make the call. It has been way too long, but he is the man for the job.

She makes the call ...but he doesn't answer. She'll have to leave a message, giving detailed directions ...no, a message is too risky.

She will call one of the others. They will know what to tell him.

She makes the call ....and she is a bit relieved. She trusts they will get in touch with him. And she has to have confidence that they will do well.

These thoughts carry more confidence than those that follow her to the hospital.

****

Meanwhile, Cindy gains some of her strength back, not in her back, but in her endurance to stay awake. And that means she and Stephen have more time to share on the phone.

Stephen is filled with questions, over the phone, "So, tell me more about Josiah. I know you've said that he's been taking care of you."

Cindy lovingly holds the phone up to her ear, in spite of the pain she is feeling, "Josiah is a wonderful young man. I know I've told you that over and over ...but you'll just have to wait to meet him. Words can't describe how wonderful he is. He's also finishing up a surprise I have for you. It would be finished by now, but, of course, all this that happened to me ...kind of rearranged things. And if I could get out of this bed, I'd be there with you right now, quarantine or no quarantine."

"I'd ask you what the surprise is, but it wouldn't be a surprise then, would it?"

Cindy laughs, "You know, I really enjoy talking with you. Do you know that we've probably talked more these past couple days—-more than we probably did for most of the combined years of our marriage? And I am so sorry for that. I know that was my fault. I was always so busy with my activities. I wish I could have slowed down back then. But I've quit all that 'running around' mentality—-I don't really know why this has happened to my back now."

"We do know why this happened to your back. Fernye needed you, and it's rather spectacular how you carried her ...you are one of a kind."

"I don't really need this messed up back at this time."

Stephen tries not to laugh, "Are you trying to say there was a time when you did need a bad back?"

Cindy tries not to laugh, because it hurts her back, "You know, it's a figure of speech. I guess I was alluding to the fact that if I'd gone through this when we were first married, maybe it would have slowed me down a bit. Okay, ...maybe not."

Stephen focuses on his own shortcomings, "And I'm sorry, I was way too tense back then. I should have been praying more for our family and working on me, instead of trying to change everyone else. But God gave me lots of time to work on that. I sure did a lot of praying over these past seventeen years."

Leah and Josiah had left early in the morning. They are going to meet Dad in a couple hours when he arrives in the state of Washington. They want to surprise their Dad.

Stephen had talked to both Leah and Josiah briefly the day before, but he hadn't asked Leah how her conference had gone. He asks Cindy at this time, "How was Leah's conference?"

"It was real good. It's important to have conferences like that. Seems most of the country no longer views abstinence as a virtue. Most follow the *Essence*, and have lost most of the standards we adhere to. Only those who still believe in Jesus, claim the full Bible standards. But, in my opinion, even they are showing signs of compromise."

"You know, Cindy, you have a lot of good ideas. I think you have an interesting and clear way of looking at things. Did you ever consider writing down your thoughts?"

XXXVII.

It is foggy. We had been at sea for so many days, we don't know if what we see, is actually what we see. The fog just adds to the shadowy mystery.

The fog feels good, breathing in this eager adventure. We are told that we are nearing the State of Washington. How long have we been staring out into the fog?

The shadow, is it an outline? Yes, an outline of land! Land ho! Suddenly we turn to the left—-and are left speechless. We are all stunned by what captures our eyes to the left. There, drifting in the fog—-it's huge! We are all taken by the immense sight. It seems almost surreal. But none of us are more taken by this than Sweeney.

Sweeney had a prized possession when he was a young boy. It was a ship in a bottle—-the kind of ship that seemed best suited for a bottle, with all your dreams bottled up inside there. Then one day he dropped the bottle. He didn't totally smash his dreams, but it didn't quite seem the same after that.

Sure, he'd play like kids will play. Once he and his brother, Murray, found an old abandoned shell of a meager rowboat. They found an old crooked stick, just long enough to use as the mast, and mom was missing some sheets off the bed for a while. When they confessed they had them, she told them to keep the sheets, she'd never be able to get them clean. They had loads of fun. But never did it come close to their real dream. Soon the dream began to fade. Sweeney had tried to hold onto his dream, but after so long, he had begun to forget it. No experience had ever gotten close to his dream—-until now. And this surpasses it!

Sweeney has goose-bumps up and down his spine. His dream had been bottled up, never to venture out. With respect to the sea, he had not abandoned his work—-though he'd abandoned his dream. He closes his eyes, then opens them again. This is five times bigger than real life. It's unbelievable!

They are all awestruck! It's kind of scary—-something that big, suddenly coming upon them from seemingly nowhere. Everyone gasps, trying to catch their breath. As they steer frighteningly close to it, Sweeney is the first to regain his breath. He hollers out, "Who owns your ship?"

An answer penetrates the fog, "Rebekkah Lessert. But this one is for a man named Murray."

Sweeney hugs his brother with wild excitement. But a lump enters his throat. This is a magnificent dream, whoever owns it. But oh, to own such a dream. He recalls her promise to get them both a ship. But he also recalls her tendency to get upset with him. Murray and Rebekkah always seem to get along, but there is something about her and Sweeney. They always seem to have a personality conflict. Maybe she'll just give him a ship in a bottle—-as a lesson to him.

The voice penetrates the fog once more, "There's one just like this one, sitting in a harbor in Maine. I was asked to take a man named Sweeney there."

Shannon exclaims, "What a dreamboat!"

Sweeney can hardly contain himself, "An 1850 Clipper ship!!"

They shore up their emotions as they go ashore. The fog has begun to lift and the day's sun glistens across the water like a sea of sparkling diamonds. Each of them seem to have their own personal journey they will be taking from this point. But first they will get themselves a good meal, and a good night's rest before saying their farewells.

A huge buffet luncheon is set up at the Hampton Inn where they will be staying overnight. But Sweeney doesn't join them.

Something isn't right. They should be here by now. He makes a couple phone calls. Well, at least they are okay. They had a little car trouble, but they'd be arriving just about sunset—-if nothing else goes wrong.

That said and done, without haste Sweeney busies himself with solidifying his connections with the gentleman who is to take him to his ship in Maine. They should both be flying out just before noon tomorrow.

The day seems to go by quickly. Evening is approaching and Murray is set to say goodbye. He is also eager to get aboard his new ship. They all gather around for a joyous farewell to Murray. The majestic sails gather in all of a soft evening breeze. As the glistening waters lose their sparkle, fading into a soft hue, the billowing sails provide a tapestry for the most beautiful of sunsets.

They are so captivated by this breathtaking view, they don't even see that their party has increased by three. Stephen still doesn't see them among the crowd, but what he can see—-he can't believe it! It looks exactly like his 1990 Transport.

Stephen gets a tear in his eye. This has to be a surprise from Cindy. She must have had it restored. They say everything now is mostly operating on hydrogen fuel cells. He had known they were experimenting with those alternate fuels—-that was no surprise. But the 1990 Transport is a surprise! It is more than nostalgic. It shows, even more, that Cindy had savored these moments shared with her husband—-even the once undesirable ones.

Stephen gazes about. Two people are standing not too far away, conspicuously so—-a young man and a young woman. He doesn't recognize them, but he feels he knows who they are.

Shannon sees that Dad has located her brother and sister, "Go ahead, Dad! Don't you recognize Leah and Josiah?"

Stephen rushes forward, but isn't as steady as he thought he was. After the first three strides, he begins to fall, but is caught by Leah and Josiah, who continue to support him for a long time with their hugs.

Stephen understands the quarantine and the final tests they had wanted to do on the boat, but now that he has a clean bill of health, why can't he just fly back? It seems unreasonable not to fly the rest of the way. He can't wait to see Cindy!

Stephen is so eager to get back home, he can't believe that they couldn't get an airline to take him back. Don't they trust that the quarantine is over? And what about Rebekkah's private jet? Is her jet not in service? He tries not to think about it any more. The old way was trying to find its way back, but Stephen wouldn't let it. He chooses not to say anything. The arrangements had been made, and for whatever reason they were made this way, he'd just accept it. No sense upsetting anyone.

Stan makes it clear he is along to volunteer his chauffeuring services. He says that Leah and Josiah should have their rest, so they can visit with their Dad on the way back home. And if not readily accepting that he'd be a good addition to the family, at least it could be seen that he's a good driver.

****

Early the next morning, they're eager and ready for their Transport to transport them back home. Shannon offers a suggestion to Dad, "How about Leah and Josiah sit on either side of you in the middle seat, so you can talk."

Stan overhears Shannon's suggestion and offers, "Will you then honor me by sitting up front?"

Shannon wants to say, "Sure", but she suddenly realizes she has not resolved her feelings towards Stan. She continues to smile, but instead answers, "I'll be up front with you about one thing ...I'm really tired, and I hope I'll be able to stretch out across the back two seats. I want to see if I can get some sleep."

As they get on their way, Dad requests, "So, Leah, tell me about this young man, our chauffeur, that you are about to marry."

* * * ** * *** * *

For the next hour, Leah talks about all the wonderful things about Stan. First of all, Dad hears all about the negotiated establishment of peace in the Middle East. He comments, "Stan, you are quite a remarkable young man! By the way, how long has our world been at peace?"

Stan explains, "Well, I know peace doesn't last forever. It seems that good feelings pass more quickly than bad. So to maintain their initial level of enthusiasm we've hired movie producer and director, Cecil B. DePasco. Each year he does a very intense personal piece ...a documentary on each of their lives. Each group so looks forward to this moment, they put all their effort into attempting to present their views and beliefs for the world to see. Of course, each group has a different way they'd like history to be written ...which places them in a more favorable light. And the truth seems to always exist somewhere in between all the different versions. But much is accomplished towards peace if we just sit down and talk ...each taking a turn to express how we feel."

Stephen remarks, "You are really quite remarkable, Stan! As our *chauffeur*, you also have much to *show for* ...as good qualities for a son-in-law."

Stan also relays some stories, which hold curious similarities to things Stephen had done, which the children must've shared with Stan.

Stephen is so consumed by the fact that Leah is about to get married, and his desire to get to know this young man ...that he shamefully engages Stan in most of the conversation. Though he has an arm around both Leah and Josiah, and continues to smile at them ...he's talked very little with his own son.

Stephen addresses Stan one more time, "The way I hear Leah speak, I am hearing the language of love. It will certainly be my honor to have you join the family, Stan."

As Stephen turns his attention to Josiah, Stan looks in the rearview mirror. Stan's eyes meet Shannon's—-and he winks. Shannon slumps in her seat and closes her eyes, pretending to sleep. What else can she do? She realizes she hasn't resolved her own feelings towards Stan. And what was that wink about? Perhaps Stan hasn't really dealt with his feelings towards her either ...but that better not be the case. She doesn't even want to think about it. She will keep her eyes closed.

An early July wedding is just around the corner. Suddenly, with the news of Dad's return, things have really changed. Time gathers together with definition and meaning. Once again there will be months and seasons. But unlike before, each day will be filled with more than just looking forward to each day. Just a short while ago those days were filled with remembering, hoping, and praying ...all good things, but there had been nothing else to fill the day. But now, memories can once again be experienced. And they can rejoice ...together.

That in itself brings meaning to the days ...spending much time together. Birthdays are always important—-and of course, their

Anniversary. Stephen had tried to memorize names of people and events—-any information that would keep his mind sharp.

Shannon reminds Dad of one date, soon to come up, that is important to her, "Father's Day is now only a couple days away," Shannon informs him. She throws her arms around him, "I'm the happiest girl in the world right now ...I have my *Poppy* back!"

Shannon crawls back into the backseat of the van. Leah and Josiah snuggle into their seats next to Dad. They had a long enough stretch. A little rest from driving for Stan ...and a bite to eat for everyone was a good idea, but now they will be on their way again.

Stan announces, "Are we ready?"

Shannon calls Mom on the cell phone. She misses Mom. But this is a moment for Mom and Dad. She hands Dad the cell phone. He talks a long time to Mom, and with all there is to talk about, it is difficult to know where to start ...and he wants her to talk about herself and their children. Cindy approaches it the same way ...as she wants him to talk about himself. And because of each wanting the other to begin talking, there is a lull in the conversation. Stephen laughs at this point, and begins announcing over the phone each mile marker they pass.

Cindy laughs as well, "I know we have lots to talk about, but when you begin announcing every mile marker, I know you are getting tired. But that's okay. From now on, I'm going to go every mile with you. But for now, I'm getting really exhausted too. I think we could both stand a little rest. How about we declare this official nap time?"

Dad announces, "Mom says it's official nap time for everyone!"
Stan smiles, "Is that so!"
Everyone laughs along with Dad, "Okay, Stan, I guess we can make an exception for you. Maybe it's best you stay awake."

****

Much distance is traveled while they are asleep. They seem to wake up all about the same time. Only Stan has an idea where they are at. He smiles, waiting for the first one to notice. Suddenly Shannon throws her arms into the air, shouting, "We're in Michigan!"

Stephen remains quiet—-a happy quiet. He tries to stay awake, but keeps dozing off. Then he falls right to sleep again, and begins to dream.

Shannon, Leah, and Josiah can't sleep. They are too eager to see how Dad responds. They had kept the walled community a secret. And it'll be a big surprise—-another extension of affections to Dad's dreams.

As they near their destination, they notice that Dad is awake, and he's beginning to look around a little more, recognizing the scenery. Metamora is an area that hasn't changed much over the years—-except for the walled community.

Dad asks, "Isn't this Metamora?"

Dad's eyes are filled with wonder and amazement. He doesn't know quite what to think of what lies before him. Then as they enter the walled community, a couple tears travel down his face.

All those years he had prayed, and hoped ...and waited. In hopeful anticipation he dreamed of being reunited with his family one day. And at the same time, through all those long years, though perhaps believing he was no longer living, they were living out his memories ...and dreams.

The tears flow. It is not only a dream, but also the property of his Mom. He reaches out, putting an arm around both Leah and Josiah, pulling them to him, resting their heads against his chest. His tears fall upon them. He is about to see Cindy again—-after all these years.

****

Cindy has Merrie Isaac braid her beautiful long hair, just the way Stephen likes it. And she also puts on the dress that she had only worn one time before. It is the dress Fernye and Stephen's Mom, Ruth, had made for her. It's the dress she'd put on over seventeen years ago—-the one she had worn for that very special surprise occasion—-that disappointed her so, when he hadn't noticed.

Yes, she recalls that time she'd wanted to break the news to him—-the news he still does not know about.

Cindy chuckles to herself. It was also the time Stephen had shaved half his face to make a point. She had felt he wasn't paying enough attention to her, yet she seldom noticed what was going on with him either.

As Cindy stitches a last stitch on the quilt she'd been rushing to finish, she closes her eyes. These small stitches are a strain on her eyes, but each stitch is like an important thread in her life.

Cindy hears a small amount of commotion. She doesn't know whether she has fallen asleep, or is about to. But now she is wide awake. She recognizes Shannon's whisper ...and quickly puts the quilt beside the sofa.

As Stephen steps into the room, it's like a moment frozen in time. He gazes lovingly into her eyes from a distance. She returns the loving glance. He knows she is unable to move about with her present back condition, but she touches him with her eyes, and her heart—-her husband is back!

Stephen kneels in front of Cindy and kisses her hand, bathing it in his tears. He can't find the words, or if he could, he can't speak them. She understands ...no words are necessary. The same unspoken love overwhelms her with tears. He sits beside her, gently moving close, kissing her again ...and again. Face-to-face, he rests his head against the back of the sofa, and looks lovingly into her eyes. He is careful to have consideration for her back, and what pain she may be in. Carefully, he moves his head closer until he rubs noses with her, before kissing her again.

They manage only a few simple words, "I love you." Then they just look at each other, speaking with the heart what words cannot express. The 'love' speaks for itself ...and that is enough.

****

Stephen is very touched by all the loving details that Cindy had preserved in his honor—-the thirty-five year old van, the walled community, and now, in all her beauty—-she is sitting upon the sofa he had knelt beside when he proposed marriage to her.

It had been Cindy's sofa, but became their sofa. Anyone else would have discarded it—-it is truly an eyesore. But talk about a sight for sore eyes—-it is not just a sofa, it contains all past tears. And now they are both drenching it in present ones—-tears of gratefulness—-falling, yet rising to new heights, within heavenly celebration. But best of all, it contains the one he truly loves—-his wife, Cindy.

Stephen looks up, and smiles. Shannon is video-taping the joyous reunion. He laughs through his tears, "Do you remember how I'd get agitated by all the video-taping? Well, I love it now ...keep taping, Shannon!"

Cindy smiles, "Your memory hasn't suffered much through all the years."

Stephen chuckles, "The memories kept me alive—-they kept me going. That's all I had! That's what helped me survive ...and prayers, of course."

Cindy wipes her tear-ridden face, "I can still remember that last day I saw you leave for work."

Stephen kisses Cindy again, "I can still see your loving face at the window, holding Josiah—-Leah holding Cody Komodo's little hand, making it wave goodbye to me—-and Shannon's toes, with faces drawn on them, also waving goodbye to me."

Shannon puts the video-camera down. Josiah and Leah join her as they kneel in front of Dad and Mom, encircling them with one big gentle group hug.

Shannon is so excited to be home again too, thinking of all the things she has missed in just the short time she's been gone—-and wanting Dad to share in everything he has missed all those years he's been gone, "Mom, can I see how you've been doing on your project?"

Cindy agrees, "Sure, I've only got a couple stitches left. Leah and Josiah can hold it up, so you and Dad can see."

They wait to hear what comments will be made. Stephen responds immediately, "That's really beautiful, dear."

Cindy smiles, looking at the children who are joining in the excitement of anticipation. Stephen suddenly bursts into a huge smile, "It's all my shirts! The designs are made from material from all my shirts!"

Cindy laughs, "I didn't know if you'd pick up on that one. Did you really miss your shirts that much?"

Stephen leans over to kiss Cindy again, "The one material clued me in. It's the same material as the shirt I wore that last day of work. How did you—-?"

Shannon laughs, holding back tears, "Everyone thought the shirt was so ugly, but you wanted to show me how much you loved me. You wore the shirt because I bought it for you. And after you disappeared, we came across the same shirt ...we just had to get it! It became my favorite shirt. I wore it all the time."

Leah and Josiah turn the quilt around. The other side is a pale blue with only one design in the very center of the quilt.

Shannon raises her eyebrows, this other side proving not to be as tastefully done. The shape looks like a pair of ...shorts? It has to be! It can't be anything else—-bright red, with white hearts?

Cindy blushes slightly, "There's a story behind that!"

Stephen's laugh is soft, mostly dominated by his big grin, "I'm sure there is a *behind* story that—-I mean, a story behind it."

Cindy blushes more by Stephen's teasing comment, "I got that material out of Fernye's keepsake box. It was with her diary. You'll have to read it sometime."

Shannon adds, "Speaking of reading—-."

Cindy acknowledges that it's not quite time yet, "That story plus many more, we were able to obtain through Fernye's diary. She turned over her keepsakes to me last year. She had a feeling this would be her last year with us. Josiah has helped me get some of the things together. He will have to show you later."

Stephen adds, "That's a good idea—-getting together some of Fernye's stories. Few people are as interesting as Fernye was."

Being the oldest child, Shannon provides some leadership, "Come on, Leah and Josiah, let's let Dad and Mom become more acquainted. Josiah, I know you probably want to get some things together at the print room. Leah, how about you join me down at the barn?"

Shannon, Leah, and Josiah depart. Shannon steps back in, just for a moment, "Sorry, I want to get the video-camera. I'm gone now."

Stephen clasps Cindy's hand within his, looking lovingly into her eyes, "I don't know where to begin ...I've missed you so much. I wanted to wait until we were alone to tell you this. I know we had a lot of struggles before I disappeared, but I want you to know that I had never stopped loving you in my heart. I definitely decreased my ability to show it, but I never stopped loving you. I'd wanted to change what we had together, and in trying to improve it, I actually made it worse. I should have just prayed about the things that bothered me so much. I don't know what I thought I was trying to do. Did I think I could change things? I see now that God did it without my help. I've painfully realized the error of my ways. I've had seventeen years to think about it. That's a lot of years to live in regret."

Cindy attempts to confess through her tears, "I've also had seventeen years to live out my regrets. But I want you to know that I felt all the prayers. I didn't know many of them were from you—-because I didn't know you were even alive. But now that I know you were there every day, praying for me, I want you to know that it wasn't easy to change. I could have easily gone more in the direction that I had already been going."

Stephen thinks back, "During all those years, since my life was so drastically changed, being alone on that island, there was much time to reflect too ...and some things became clearer to me, while other things just continued to be confusing. I kept thinking back to those last days before I disappeared ...over and over, feeling there was something I was missing that you had been trying to tell me. It was probably God telling me how much I'd missed out on as a result of my failure to change *my* ways."

Cindy looks into his eyes, "We'll have lots of time now, to tell each other so many of the things."

There are more tears than words. There is much, much more to be said, but hopefully the separation is behind them, and now they can be together in a way they weren't ...even when they were together.

It doesn't seem like it, but another hour passes. These moments are timeless.

Cindy has some very important things she has yet to share, "My Doctor told me that I can try walking on my own in a few days, but I don't ever want to walk on my own again. I don't ever want to be separated from you, not even for a minute. Though I guess I can part with you a few minutes, if you'll gather up our children, so we can eat. Josiah is probably still at the print room. It's attached to the church ...you can't miss it. Then he can take you to the barn, where the others should be at."

Stephen finds Josiah busy at work in the print room. Josiah stops his work to express a few words, "There were some things I wanted to say to you, but I wanted to wait until we had a moment alone. Growing up without a Dad was not easy, but Mom did the best she could. She's done a wonderful job with us. I can't imagine having a better Mom. But I know you prayed for us every day too, so I want you to know that I know that has been a big part too. I didn't know you were praying, but I'm sure it made a big difference. I want to thank you for that."

Josiah has a book in his hand. As Stephen embraces Josiah in another big hug, he can feel the book press against his back. But mostly he can feel the love shared between a father and a son. He had wondered how easily he'd be able to become a part of Josiah's life, but he can see now that there will be no problem bridging the gap the years had created.

Stephen cries tears of thanksgiving, "Mom is so right, you've become a wonderful young man, and I'm so happy God has blessed me with two wonderful daughters—-and a son."

They hug for a moment longer, then Josiah hands Dad the book that had been pressing against his back.

Stephen reads aloud: "The Essence."

Josiah explains, "It's not actually my project. I'm just helping Mom. She says I'm quite good at operating the printing machines."

Tears begin to flow again as Stephen turns the pages. It's the story he had begun before their marriage—-and Cindy had found his notes, and written out the story. Now this is the most loving gesture of all.

Beyond words, there have been so many loving gestures. And the entire family has helped to contribute. But, Cindy had not only organized all this, Stephen is amazed at how much work Cindy had actually put into it herself. Stitching the quilt must have been really time consuming. She must have really slowed down her busy schedule to make time for that. Of course, she has been kind of forced by the doctor's orders to stay home lately. But, she had to have begun the writing quite some time ago. It takes no small commitment. Of all the unbelievable things Cindy has done in honor of her husband, this is the greatest.

Josiah adds, "Mom says this is the first part, but it doesn't end here. We are all eager to continue the story as our lives continue together—-and she's going to continue writing."

Stephen is speechless. He doesn't know what to say. The book also contains stories of each of the children. He turns a few pages ... to the Thanksgiving skit. He definitely remembers that one. He reads aloud:

"After the skit, Cindy pleads with me to never ever get the children politically involved ...so I then begin teaching them the Ten Commandments instead. Leah and Josiah are so close in age, they're always doing things together. Most of the time they are wonderful together, and I love to see them play. But as with any children, the process of 'together' can lead into areas which we call their personal growth, if they're ready and willing to accept their differences—-which all children have."

Stephen reads what is perceived to have been his motive:

"I wanted to make sure the children understood that Jesus died for our sins ...and by understanding His love and forgiveness, we can better conceptualize the forgiveness we are to extend to one another. Josiah asks, 'What is sin?' I explain, 'Sin is going against God, and going against His provision for us.' I know that I'm not speaking entirely at their level, so that's when I decide that I will go through the Ten Commandments with them ...covering only one commandment each day. The first three days are spent describing who God is to us—-recognizing, respecting, and responding. The children seem to understand the fourth commandment quite well. The fifth day I discuss with them what some parents errantly stress as even more important than the first three: Honor Your Parents. I also mention that it works best if Dad and Mom also honor each other. For the sixth day, the question of war comes up, but I try not to get political. That evening I have to work overtime at work ...and it feels like a war. I am so worn out, but the children are so enthusiastic, so I begin reading, not knowing what trouble I'm about to get into ...until the words leave my lips, 'Do Not Commit Adultery'. I am so tired, I don't really feel like doing this. Probably wouldn't be any better though, even if I wasn't tired. Maybe it's better that I am tired ...I don't really think before I speak. For some strange reason, I take an environmentalist point of view, 'Do not *come at* an adult tree. Remember when we planted that baby apple tree in our front yard, well, now it's an *adult tree* ...and it has apples.' Leah asks, 'Why is that a sin?' I explain, 'Well, God created for us, every good fruit. And we shouldn't just chop it down.' Josiah adds, 'Like George Washington did with the cherry tree?' I yawn, 'Something like that ...we just need to save our trees. And it is fruitless to chop them down. Believe me, if we don't 'come-at *adult trees*, we save a lot.' I end by promising to plant more baby apple trees with them ...some other day."

Before Dad reads too much, Josiah suggests, "I don't know about you, but I'm hungry. How about we go down to the barn and get the others? They are beginning to serve at the church cafeteria, where everyone in the walled community eats together, but ours will be brought to the house, since Mom can't get around. Besides, we want you all to ourselves for these first few days."

They find Shannon and Leah in a horse pen. Shannon is feeding a baby colt a bottle, "The mother is sick, so we have to bottle feed this one."

Leah adds, " That's why I like the barn. It's so full of the real things in life."

Shannon's face lights up, as she always does telling horse stories, "This colt is sired by Breeze—-just before Rebekkah had Breeze shipped to the islands, this little one was in the making. It's truly remarkable how that happens, isn't it?"

Stephen leans on the fence. Shannon stands up, "Dad, I'd like you to meet the young man who's been taking care of these precious horses while I've been gone."

A young man wearing a captain's hat, steps into view carrying a bail of hay in each hand—-the twine taut between straining fingers at the end of down-stretched arms.

Stephen playfully interrupts, "Now don't tell me ...you look to be the age of Dave and Sherry's boy. You must be ...Jonah Stage."

The young man answers with his back turned, as he carries the bails of hay into an adjacent stall, "No, you've got my age figured fairly well, but Jonah is a year older than me."

Stephen steps over to the stall and leans on the rail, "Okay, now I've got it ...Ray and Claudia Isaac were due to have a child in late fall, of 2008. They didn't know whether they'd have a boy or girl, but you must be that blessed son."

Stephen extends a hand, "Glad to meet you, Sir, I'm Stephen Razohn ...Dad to Shannon, Leah, and Josiah."

The young man extends his hand and shakes hands, "I'm Samuel Isaac."

Stephen smiles, "Well, I'll have to tell Ray and Claudia what a fine young man they have, next time I see them. Last time I saw your folks, your mom was beginning to show you quite well, at 7 to 8 months. It's a pleasure now, to meet you officially."

Samuel declares, "I don't mean to confuse you, but I'm not Ray and Claudia's son ...my middle name is Isaac, not my last name. But Ray and Claudia did have a boy—-and he is a fine young man, as well as a friend of mine. His name is Aidin Isaac."

Stephen smiles, "This is interesting. Now let me see, if I have your age right, and you're not Ray and Claudia's boy—-"

Samuel shakes the chaff off his captain's hat and relocates it on his head, with the brim not so close to his eyes this time. He is so filled with emotion, he tries not to tremble with his words, "I'll give you a small hint. I was one of the first to move into the walled community with my Mom. Dad, on the other hand, just recently moved in."

Stephen admits, "Well, that may be a hint, but I'm sorry, I don't have a clue. I don't know of anyone else who was to have a child, so I probably don't know your family. I wasn't even around when this community first opened."

Strangely, Stephen feels drawn to this young man, "Were your parents separated for very long?"

Samuel looks into Stephen's caring eyes, then quickly looks away, "Yes, quite a while."

Stephen senses this young man is still feeling the pain, "I'm sorry to hear that. But it's good they're together again—-you're happy for that, right?"

Samuel looks back into his eyes, "Yes, Mom really loves Dad."

Stephen seems to fall quickly into the mental health routine. It's been years, but he still has it within him. He has a natural caring for people and their situations, "Do you think Dad loves Mom?"

Samuel looks deeper into his eyes, "Yes, I believe so."

Stephen searches further, "Do you love your Dad?"

Samuel glances away temporarily, then looks back, "I've only been able to spend a few minutes with my Dad, but I do believe I love him. I guess I was hesitant because I wasn't sure how he feels about me."

Stephen tries to reassure the young man, "Well, if Mom loves Dad, and you believe Dad truly loves Mom—-then I'm sure he loves you too. And with the kind of special young man I've been talking to for the past few minutes, I can't imagine it would take long. You just have to spend time together. I've been separated from my entire family for quite some time. We've just recently got back together—-and it's been the best. But we were separated under different circumstances, so I'm not going to say it's always easy. Some things take time. But time is usually in our favor. Time often allows the best of things to heal."

Samuel looks directly at Stephen, "I'll agree to give it a try. My circumstances aren't really that different from what you described."

Stephen extends his hand again, "Well, my wife is waiting to have dinner with the four of us, so we'd better go. Maybe you and your folks could join us some time."

Samuel shakes his hand, "I'd like that."

Stephen smiles, "Good. I'll make a point to look up your folks. Nice meeting you, Samuel."

Stephen turns to leave, then turns back around, "Oh, silly me, I forgot to ask your last name."

Samuel stares ahead with wonder, his eyes growing bigger, "My last name is Razohn—-Samuel Isaac Razohn, Sir ...I mean, Dad."

Stephen is frozen, for only a moment, as he takes in what was just said. Then it suddenly all clicks ...that's what she'd tried to tell him before he disappeared!

Stephen rushes forward with open arms, tearfully embracing the son he didn't even know existed. Cindy's deep love—-her greatest gesture of all, proving to be the greatest Father's Day surprise. And she'd chosen the very name he had picked out for Josiah, with the initials, S.I.R.—-Sir.

Stephen continues to embrace Samuel—-and tears are not only spent by him, but by Samuel as well. All that pent-up anticipation, wondering if he'd be accepted as the others were accepted, is now released and able to find a resting place—-a place of security and contentment.

****

They all arrive back as Merrie Isaac is delivering the meal. Stephen kisses Cindy, then is somewhat successful getting out the words, "That was the best surprise of all ...I love you so much."

Stephen gets choked up in tears. He had cried at funerals, but this is the most he had ever cried in his life—-and they are all tears of joy.

Merrie also directs Shannon's attention to a package that had just arrived. It is from Indonesia. Shannon picks up the small package and reads, "It's from Tevita."

It is addressed to her, so she opens it. Inside the package is Cody Komodo.

XXXVIII.

More tears fall—-but these are not mere tears of joy. An entire community—-and beyond, of all the people who knew Rebekkah over the years, most will not visit her gravesite.

No one was more loved than Fernye at the walled community. Tears will continue to be spent for Fernye ...her gravesite standing as a garden, a floral delight.

But for Rebekkah, it will be different ...she was different. She hadn't shared her struggles with anyone ...she'd downplayed a mild heart attack, and had not even mentioned the stroke. Then she'd pretended to be fine, when she knew she was not. She hadn't even asked for prayer. And she wasn't even really Rebekkah ...she was Sarah Tressel.

For Rebekkah, it will certainly be different—-merely by the fact of the strange nature of people themselves. There's a sort of strange attraction towards the 'Rebekkah-type' ...the closed-up, private, and unrevealing self. The intrigue and wonderment is often towards those who we can't quite figure out. But the fact that probably draws so much attention—-is a sad fact, indeed. Not by her deeds, but by what will be in her 'deed'.

What will be in her deed will be revealed later today. As they leave the cemetery proceeding to the church within the walled community, there is a meal being prepared. After they eat, they will view a video-tape Rebekkah had prepared. She had been very popular in the Seattle area as an anchorwoman, but that was a while ago. It had been Rebekkah's choice to leave the station, but a new popular person had taken her place. And she felt it wouldn't be long before she'd be forgotten.

Most people in the walled community knew Rebekkah to be confident and influential. They also imagine she had done well financially, and they knew she was friends with George Olitz ...but, that's about all they knew.

Maggie knows more than most others, even more than her husband. She had wished she hadn't, but she had agreed not to tell of Rebekkah's secrets. Her husband, Stephen Tressel, knew of the wealth he had inherited ...but he had trusted George, whom he knew had been handling the tremendous wealth. He felt the corporate world provides jobs for people, and that is a good thing. And he had made it clear that the small arm of R&S Corporation was more than sufficient to handle his needs. And in truth, that involved millions ...but it's still negligible compared to all the investments made over the years, contributing to the Tressel estate.

Most of the people who knew that Rebekkah was actually Sarah, are all in Heaven ...and aside from Maggie, who on earth knows? George had known ...but he knows very little now, with his health fading fast.

Cindy shares in the sadness, yet feels slightly better physically. She has Stephen gently escort her to the gravesite, then assist her into a chair provided for her near the grave. Leah stands beside her and the rest of the family, all in line alongside the casket. Stan stands on the other side of Stephen.

Stephen puts a hand on Stan's shoulder, speaking in a low respectful tone, "These are difficult moments—-but I'm looking forward to being a part of a more joyous occasion."

Stan realizes this may be the beginning of the 'big talk'. He looks into Stephen's eyes and speaks first, "I know it's proper to ask—-so, I'd like to officially ask for your daughter's hand in marriage. I know we've already made plans to marry in a couple weeks, but you weren't around for me to ask. So, I'm asking now."

Stephen looks off in the distance, "You know, I do seem to remember a time I did a skit for the children about this very thing."

Stan smiles, "Yes, it *rings* familiar with me too. Your family has shown me the video-tape of a skit you once did. I've seen it on more than one occasion. You said that no one loves your daughters as much as you do—-except God. But if you're convinced that a person is God's choice, you will allow them to get a ring."

Stephen pats Stan on the back, then drops his hand back to his side. He looks to the crowd around him, gathered around Rebekkah's gravesite, "Yes, God's choice—-and to know it. Many parents take a step of faith along with their children when this choice time arrives. Those children leave two people they know love them for who they are—-for someone who hasn't proven themselves yet. I guess what I'm trying to say ...is for you not to value the gift over the *Giver*. For instance, Shannon has always spoken as if there's no greater gift than a horse, yet she values me more. And I believe that horse will be happier on that island than I ever was."

Stephen smiles, then adds, "Now, I hear a couple years ago you had considered marrying Shannon. Whether it was Shannon then, or Leah now—-my point is the same."

Stan gets an uncomfortable feeling. He interrupts, "I don't know how you mean exactly. I do know you're considering giving Leah to me in marriage—-that's a great gift. But I don't really know you. I'm sorry, but I can't value you over Leah. That seems strange to even ask. I mean no disrespect, Sir, but I've never heard of such a thing."

Stephen feels like he is suddenly the one on the outside ...he's the one who has been gone all these years. Leah is probably more comfortable with Stan than she is with her own Dad. And this 'big talk' idea is perhaps not such a good idea.

There is nothing he can probably say to add hope or clarity to their lives anyway. But he has to at least try to fix what he has already said. Stephen breathes deeply, "I didn't mean *me* ...I mean God, the *Giver of life*. With those who leave God for something else, that's considered foolishness. But, together if you step out with faith that God will lead you, I guess that needs no proof. God will do the proof through you. But with you, Stan, I guess you've proven yourself to the entire world, and they all love you—-so, I guess mine doesn't demand as great a faith."

Stephen knows what he's trying to say, even if he isn't able to stumble through it. But of all the things he had thought about on the island, he hadn't rehearsed this one. It's just that ...that he was so used to picturing Shannon, Leah, and Josiah ...the age they were before he'd disappeared. But he will have to get used to the fact that they're grown now. After all, Cindy certainly had 'trained them up in the way they should go'.

Cindy can't help recalling some of her and Stephen's past failures. Her sincere hope is that Leah was too young at the time to be affected. She prays Leah will not repeat some of those same tendencies in her own marriage.

Cindy offers some advice, "Leah, you can make a difference. I hope you don't repeat my failures. Don't busy yourself or let others busy you, for that matter. You have to learn how to manage your time. If you don't, you'll each get frustrated and begin fighting against what God gave you—-each other. You'll become tense and unsatisfied—-arguing much of the time. You can drive down even a good man that way. I know I did."

Leah glances over at Dad, who is talking to Stan. Then she turns back her attention to Mom, who has more to say, "Not having enough time is a bad thing. Most people would say you need time away from the children too—-to be by yourself. I believe that too much emphasis can be put on that. A husband and wife should be able to enjoy each other's company with the children present too." Cindy puts an arm around Leah, "And don't make the mistake

I did. Most people don't want to admit it, but one of the main culprits can be excessive church activity."

As the meal is finished, they depart the cafeteria area and seat themselves in the church pews. There is an awkward quietness. The walled community is a unique place, and part of that uniqueness had been provided by Rebekkah.

Not many people are surprised. Those whom Rebekkah deeply cared about had likely already had conversations with her about not wanting to be beneficiaries. That was likely the stance Stephen and Aleah had taken; the two she'd acted like *Grandma* to. Their point of view was to let business be business, and let love be love.

Within the ranks of the dozen corporate heads, CEOs of businesses that Rebekkah owned, they all had seen George as her favorite, not only sharing her business sense, but also her unique philosophies of life. For many years now, in the business world, most everyone seemed to anxiously anticipate George would likely eventually marry Rebekkah. That hadn't happened, but surely the trust they had between them was going to keep intact their common corporate goals.

Lately, much has changed in the corporate world—-but, all the changes only made Rebekkah more dominant. The government intervened and tried to split some of her corporate influence, but they had failed.

Also failing though, was George's health. At first he showed the beginning signs of dementia ...but it got much worse. George's failing health brought increased communication by the other corporate heads. They began vying for preferred positions. This shifty shifting was not visible to those in the walled community ...nor did they care. But they did care about George, and his condition began to degenerate even more quickly, the general diagnosis being Alzheimer's disease. The business world would have a difficult time accepting the fact that everything was still in George's hands. He certainly couldn't manage it. Then the answer became obvious ...he hadn't been.

George had been slowly turning it over into the capable hands of Stan. No one has more proven ability than Stan. And Rebekkah would not just be turning over the crucial business dealings to a stranger—-it would be in the caring and capable hands of a friend. Absolutely no one was more cherished than Stan in the walled community—-perhaps in the entire world. And no one loved Stan more than Leah. And within their loving community, everyone was considered an integral part of their close-knit church family.

Stan waits until most have departed. Then he leads Leah over to her Dad's side. There is something he feels he needs to tell both Leah and her parents. Stan chooses his words carefully, "That's going to be an exciting trip. Rebekkah had certainly planned well—-with each of you lovingly in mind."

Stephen speaks not only for himself, but the rest of the family as well, "We aren't going on any trip. We have a wedding to attend in a couple weeks."

Stan hesitates, finding it difficult to form his words, "George is quickly getting worse. I'd find it extremely difficult for me to enjoy the beginnings of my marriage, when I could possibly be losing him. He's been the best dad—-more than I can imagine a dad could ever be. He needs me now. And you've all just lost Fernye—-and now Rebekkah. But beyond that, there is an even more important consideration."

Stan turns most of his attention to Leah, though he is still speaking to the entire family, "Leah, I really feel you need to spend this time with your Dad. He has just found his way back into your life, and you both have so much lost time to make up. I love you so much, Leah—-and I want to marry you soon. I want to spend our lives together. I feel that is the direction our lives are going—-and that is an irreversible direction. I love you now—-and I always will. My love for you grows day by day. And though I know our direction will never change, within our path is a short detour. It has been clearly marked for both of us. You should spend this time with your Dad and I should spend this time with mine. My love for you can only grow stronger. One of the big reasons I love you so much is the fact that you are always compelled to do what is right. And I'm confident you'll agree that this is the right thing to do. In your heart, I think you know this is the direction to go. So go on the trip that Rebekkah has provided for you and your family. My heart will never leave you. So, go—-and when you get back, we will get married."

Leah is filled with tears. She does not speak.

Stan feels very awkward, not knowing what Leah is thinking. He doesn't know what else to say, but he feels compelled to say more, "When difficulty comes our way, it can distract us, and help us lose our goal, but oftentimes it can help us meet it. I feel the first step in professing my commitment to you is in taking a step back at this time—-so you and your family can be available to one another during this time of grieving. It's not actually a step backward, but a step forward."

Leah hugs Stan, then finally finds the words through her tears, "I know you'd say something like that. Do you know why? Because you have the same love that Dad has. That's why I want to marry you. I love you even more for what you just said. But I have to let you know, it will not be easy. What you are asking of me at this moment, is to do the most difficult thing I've ever done—-to let go. I love you so much ...I don't really want to go, but I know you are right. I know I need to go. But I want you to know, the entire time I'll be thinking of you, and looking forward to the day I return."

They hug, then extend their arms, holding each other still, and looking into each other's eyes. Leah's tears sparkle, "In a couple weeks, Dad and I will be walking all over Israel, walking the very ground Jesus walked on. But the walk I look most forward to with Dad, is the one down the aisle, to be united in the Name of Jesus, with you."

****

Stan wants to be there for the farewell when Leah boards the plane, but that won't be for several hours yet. He should have enough time to visit George first.

They had just finished eating, and they are seated in a room adjacent to the dining room. Soft piano music is providing an atmosphere of quiet relaxation. As the music ends, the atmosphere becomes rather quiet. Few people are compelled to hold any actual conversation at all. Stan is one of them. He sits silently beside George.

With quiet excitement, an elderly man enters the room. His eyes quickly search about, before locating Stan from across the room. The man appears to be in his mid-80's, but has a definite youthfulness about him. His vibrancy is so evident, it captivates the attention of everyone. Even those who appeared to be asleep are suddenly awakened to the fact that someone uniquely different has just entered their presence. It appears to be an almost subconscious awareness.

The man approaches Stan, "Hi, my name is Andrew Bray ...are you, Stan Olitz?"

But before he can answer, a man about Stan's age turns to the two of them, voicing his frustration aloud, "How do you do it? You sit here for hours ...and they don't even know who you are!"

Andrew smiles softly with compassionate eyes, and a heart that fills the emptiness of the entire room, "But we know who they are ...don't we?"

He hesitates before continuing, "My wife stuck with me when I went into the Air Force. Her prayers flew overhead every night. We had children at the time. I counted on her quiet commitment to me and the children ...it gave me strength during times I fear I would not have survived. I had others by my side ...while she battled alone. She gave it her all ...and that strong commitment has always brought great meaning to my entire life. The good Lord has shown me so much through her. My wife's work is now done ...but she is very much alive. She represents all of who I am ...and who I could ever hope to be. Without her, I would not have experienced such depths of love. I come here in quiet appreciation and gratitude."

****

As they are about to board the plane, everyone is ready, except Leah. Where is Stan? She thinks aloud, "He said he'd be here to see us off."

She looks about in desperation, wondering what can be wrong. She knows Stan certainly would be here ...unless something had gone dreadfully wrong.

Then Stan steps into view. And what Leah sees, she had never seen before ...Stan is crying.

Leah hugs Stan, as if it were a forever goodbye hug. She holds him close and looks upward into his eyes. Though the tears are beginning to clear up, they are something she'll cling onto forever.

Those tears are solely for her. No one had ever seen Stan cry before—-but she feels that's because God had preserved the most precious tears for this moment—-for her.

Josiah is not insensitive to this, yet he is feeling the sensitivity of his stomach, not his heart. Besides, how long can a hug go on? And he feels the longer it goes on, the more chance it will.

He has a humorous, sort of practical, way about him, "Let's eat—-I'm starved! They can't serve us until we are in flight. And I hear they have an awesome steak and onion sandwich. I don't know why I'm thinking about that, I don't even like onions. I just have this olfactory sensation. I must really be hungry."

Samuel smiles at Josiah and nudges him, "Be more sensitive to what your sister is going through. Think with your heart, not your stomach."

This brings laughter to the group. Stan and Leah break their hug and join in with the laughter, but Leah still holds onto Stan's hands, as she faces him for this difficult farewell. She pulls him towards her one last time—-and kisses him, then quickly departs, boarding the plane as tears streak her face.

As the plane stabilizes in flight, they begin to serve the meal. Samuel teases, "You must have been hungry, Josiah. You were beginning to hallucinate. They don't even serve a steak and onion sandwich."

Josiah smiles, "I must have been thinking about that restaurant in the airport. When we walked past it, they were chopping the vegetables right there in the corridor as we were passing by. Probably to get us to buy one of their sandwiches. You know, it really works. The onion smell was so strong, it almost made me cry."

Samuel looks over the menu, "I'm going to cry if they don't have my specialty."

Josiah reaches into his carry-on bag of books, pulling out a zip-lock bag with a peanut butter and dill pickle sandwich inside. He hands it to Samuel.

Samuel grins with delight, "You are such a sensitive brother. Never again will I accuse you of being insensitive."

As they enter the clouds, 'cloud nine' now seems to be the most prominent—-the nine of them looking forward to their destination in Israel. Meanwhile, everyone is content with enjoying each other's company—-except the pilot and co-pilot.

Ken is grateful that Rebekkah had arranged for him to go along with his daughter and her family. Ken had never been to Israel before and he's eager to visit the Holy Land. Though the co-pilot isn't reflecting that same eagerness as he motions to Ken.

As Ken leaves his seat and approaches the co-pilot, he sees the concerned look on the co-pilots face. He and the co-pilot talk, then the co-pilot returns to join the pilot.

Ken returns to his seat, but remains standing, to get their attention, "Some difficulty has been sighted—-and as always, a precautionary measure takes top priority. Therefore, we are going to have to land prematurely. We are getting clearance to land. The pilot will have to turn the plane around, but we are not that far from Toronto."

Ken returns to his seat after reassuring them that everything will be okay. But he is actively talking on his cell phone to someone.

Upon landing, Ken continues to act as the spokesperson, having communicated to someone on the ground, "We won't be able to continue on with our plane. They'll have to spend a couple days checking it out, so we have a couple options—-we can wait a couple days, or arrange another flight. So it's either a couple days or several hours. Either way, we're stuck here right now. But because of our inconvenience, a tour of Toronto has been provided, compliments of our airline."

They are provided a 7-seat van. Cindy is getting around okay, with Stephen's arm always there to support her. She comfortably seats herself next to her husband after everyone else loads in, "Okay, I'm ready."

And at that cue, the van is on its way.

Ken drives them from the airport. Suddenly, they hear a rather large explosion.

Cindy, Shannon, and Leah all seem to speak at once, "What was that!"

Stephen, Josiah, and Samuel are more composed. Josiah speaks up, "Probably just some fireworks. You know, the 4th of July is only a few days away."

Samuel adds, "Isn't the 4th of July—-a celebration of our Independence? I don't think Canada, with their French and Indian populations, would celebrate in the same sort of way."

Josiah counters, "Do you think Toronto really cares how they celebrate? I think they just like to celebrate. They'll join anyone when—-*It's time to party!*"

Ken is thankful for Josiah's comments. The questions cease for the time being.

Only Stephen makes one more reference about it, "I'd rather no fireworks at all. It landed me seventeen years. I'll celebrate the day when there are no fireworks."

Ken offers an explanation, "I know I said a tour of Toronto has been arranged—-well, the plan was not to tour all of Toronto. I'm actually going to take you directly to what I consider the best part."

Ken drives them to the waterfront. And there—-is the most beautiful sight to be seen. Shannon announces excitedly, "Mom! Leah, Josiah, Samuel—-look! Is this your surprise, Grandpa? It must be Sweeney!"

Ken smiles, "Yes, Shannon—-and it is every bit as beautiful as you'd described."

Ken parks the van and Sweeney greets them, "Come on, I'll take you on board."

Sweeney takes them to a motor boat, and they all hop in to get an 'on board' look at his Clipper ship. He announces, "We are expecting another bus load of people, then I'll raise the sails for you. But until they get here, you might as well let me take you on the official tour."

Upon completing the tour, they look ashore.

Sweeney announces, "The bus has arrived. As soon as the others get aboard, we'll raise these sails. It's quite a spectacular sight ...an experience you won't soon forget."

As the motorboat brings the first load of passengers, Cindy is the first to notice, "Jesse, Mrs. Odakota,—-Merrie Isaac, Charles, Ray and Claudia, Aidin—-Dave and Sherry, Jonah ...."

Sweeney smiles, "When I told them I was in Toronto, the entire community decided to come out for a tour. I guess they can all thank Jesse. He is quite the convincing young man. I don't think anyone will be disappointed."

A few more trips with the motorboat—-and everyone is on board.

Leah doesn't tell anyone, but she is looking for Stan. She is hoping for that surprise. Stan has a nurse helping with George, so perhaps Stan could spare a few hours away. It would be a nice surprise—-but it would be impossible. The bus would have had to have left the walled community well before her plane had taken off. Leah realizes her sweet dream is not possible. She gives up looking for Stan—-then she finds him!

XXXIX.

One of the shipmates is watching the news—-and there is Stan, on the television screen. Leah steps closer to the television ...to see the close-up of Stan and hear what the report says:

"When I returned from bidding farewell to my fiancée at the airport, I returned to find my dad had passed away. Then I find out that the plane my fiancée is on had to make an emergency landing. The plane exploded, but they can't say whether everyone was able to exit the plane in time. I'm having a hard enough time with Dad's passing—-and I desperately need to know whether my fiancée and her family are okay. So, Leah, please call me! Or if anyone knows where Leah is, please contact me!"

Leah locates Grandpa immediately and asks to use his cell phone. Ken can see the desperation in his granddaughter's eyes as he hands her the phone.

Stan answers quickly. He was certain Leah would call him right away. Leah gives him reassurance that everyone is okay, then she extends her sympathy to Stan in the loss of his dad. She tells Stan she is going to make arrangements to return home, to be by his side at his dad's funeral.

Ken is talking to Jesse—-when Leah interrupts, "Grandpa, can you tell Stan where exactly it is that we're at. He says he's going to come pick me up. After George's funeral, he said he and I can join the rest of you in Israel."

Jesse grabs the phone instead, "I know exactly where we're at—-I can give him directions."

Jesse walks to the other end of the ship with the cell phone, talking for several minutes. When he returns to Leah, the phone call had ended, "Stan had to go. He has much to do with funeral arrangements. I explained to him that it would take twice as long for him to drive out here and back, so no sense in him driving here when I can drive you back in half the time. But I'd like to first see what I came out here to see. It should take less than an hour."

Leah wipes her tears, "I guess, that's reasonable. I'm sure he has much on his mind with George's passing. I wouldn't want him to have to drive all the way out here. Thanks, Jesse."

Jesse hands the phone back to Ken, "Just before Stan hung up with me, he said thanks Ken. This cell phone doesn't give very good reception, but then again, some people just think I sound like you."

Jesse turns to Leah, "Leah, you didn't even mention that the rest of us were here, or that you were on board Sweeney's Clipper ship."

Leah thought it was obvious, "Stan just lost his dad. I wasn't going to mention what fun we were having. And to be honest, I'm not having any fun. But I don't want to ruin it for the rest of you. Let's see if they are ready for the presentation. And I don't mean to rush you, but I am eager to get back home."

Sweeney explains that there is a 15-minute movie on the making of the Clipper ship. Then he will proceed on with the spectacular event—-the raising of the sails.

Leah is in a daze ...thinking only about Stan. She is paying no attention to the movie about the Clipper ship—-until five minutes into the movie. That's when Rebekkah comes on, over the screen. That grabs Leah's attention.

Rebekkah's taped words are rather haunting, "You've all had the opportunity to see the first version of my last will and testament. Now, I'd like you to view another version. The last time I talked with you, I merely explained to everyone about how I'd dispense my fortune. Things will not change. As they say, it will be 'business as usual'. But now, I will further detail the *why* aspect of my decision. George, I know you are deteriorating quickly. And you probably won't even understand ...... "

XL.

Often people question what they are asked to do. Sweeney had been following orders, without question, for most of his life. On the inside, he had questioned just about everything, but had not dared to outwardly challenge his dad. He had a very dominant dad. Dads often teach their sons the work ethic, along with the game of economics, but Sweeney's dad had overdone it. And Sweeney didn't just feel trapped during those long childhood years, the grip remained tight upon him in adulthood also. Then Christianity gripped him. He imagined things would be different. This trip would be the last time he would subject himself to following orders in this manner. He had resolved to follow a higher order.

Sweeney doesn't see a conflict of commitment here. And the confusion that will follow, will not be something he will have to answer to. His hopes are that everything will go as planned ...and no one will even suspect him.

Stan does not know what to think. But he soon has plenty to think about. He has just received a copy of the same movie, minus the Clipper ship segment. George is no longer alive, but if he had been, he had deteriorated too far to have been able to understand it. Rebekkah had guessed right about that.

Stan's emotions are all over the map, but he is a composed person. Before panic sets in, he resolves to not let this thing defeat him. He will use what knowledge he has to his advantage. It will drive him even more to pursue his goals. He will not disappoint George. He will live on, with the common purpose George had taught him. And what Rebekkah had expected of him, he will do.

Stan had expected Leah to be by his side, but she is not. Yes, he had told her to go on the trip, but when George passed away, she had said she was coming back. But, she is not here. Something had happened! Now, Stan stands at George's gravesite—-alone.

So much has happened. He has just lost his dad, now he has to have closure with that. George had been sick for some time. He'd prepared for this day …many times over in his mind. But now, this ordeal with Leah—-he had not prepared for that.

Stan won't rest until he knows what has happened—-where she is at. He will send out another televised plea, like the one he had sent out when the plane had blown up. It hadn't taken long before she had let him know she survived. He hopes for the same success this time. If he doesn't hear from her he will have the entire nation looking for his fiancée.

This is maddening. Just like the disappearance of Leah's dad, thought to have been solved, yet now proven to be unsolved for seventeen years—-now, Leah is missing and there is no word where she is.

With the passing of both George and Rebekkah, Stan has become perhaps the most powerful person in the world. But how fragile is that? What does one have to gain, or what does one stand to lose?

As the world sees it, Stan had lost his dad and now possibly, Leah. They reach out with their heartfelt sympathy. But they don't really know what he is really going through. And so far, they have not been successful in helping him find Leah.

This does not just involve one nation. Leah and her family had disappeared in Canada. That makes it an international search.

But no nation, not even the world, can know what he is going through—-or what he is yet to go through.

* * * * ***** * * * ***** * * * * *

Weeks pass by. It is not just Leah missing, but the entire residents of their walled community. And Stan contemplates the disturbing connection. He prides himself in his acute ability to see things in advance. He had always felt suspect about the walled community concept. They act like cows, following each other down a path ...a path they accept without question. Stan has so many questions though. And the biggest of these questions has him asking himself where he can place his trust. Yet, the answer is quite clear. There is always money. Money can help him get what he wants. Even if a few things stand in the way—-even if things may temporarily look unfavorable—-money will work things out where otherwise there may be no hope. It worked for Rebekkah, now it can work for him. The only problem with Rebekkah was that she had begun to give up. But he won't! He will pursue his goal to the end.

The nation does not have enough time to react to what Stan is going through, when they get hit with their own devastating blow. East coast, West coast, South, and Midwest—-from Washington D.C., to San Francisco, New Orleans, and Chicago. It so happens that Stan is in the nation's Capitol at the time ...and he is also diagnosed as having—-Smallpox.

Stan had just negotiated another merger with his company when fear makes its bid. The government has word that it's not a terrorist act. The world is still experiencing an unprecedented period of peace. They are still honoring the peace he had helped to negotiate. They love him. Everyone loves him. That's why the entire world reaches out with concern at this time. No one seems ready to accept the fact that their leader—-their hero, may not survive.

There are those in our country who are trained in finding answers, when questions become overwhelming. They often race against the clock to find answers. And this is no exception.

They track the origin of this smallpox. There had been a fire at one of the facilities where it was kept on file, in case there was ever an outbreak of the disease. That area of the building was not affected by the fire, but they had decided to move everything. Stan had called a meeting of the CEOs of many loyal businesses within various cities to meet with his many scientists. Then Stan travels to Washington D.C. on business. That's when the smallpox rears its ugly head.

Stan addresses the nation to dispel fears of terrorism. From his hospital bed, he convinces the nation that the world still has a strong resolve for peace. He explains how the smallpox had leaked, but now is under control. He does not have to explain how weak he is—-they can see that. The world stands by, hoping Stan will make it. They also rely on his strength of character to help them get through.

Stan's final words are, "Leah, my dear, if you can somehow hear me out there, please send word that you are okay. I love you!"

Those were Stan's final televised words, though not his final words. Though having to endure the painful struggle, Stan does make it through. And he still clings onto that faint hope that Leah will make it through ...that she'll contact him.

The nation comes together in prayer. They pray that the Essence will stand by Stan, and heal him. And they also pray that Leah will be found.

XLI.

Stan eventually does get better, but still no word of, or from Leah. The President of the United States is kneeling beside a little girl, about the age of four, in a hallway at the White House. He comforts her amid all those bright lights and cameras. The President then introduces the little girl to the television audience, "This is my daughter, Joslyn. We call her Joss."

The President takes Joss by the hand and leads her through a set of double doors, "We have two guests waiting here. The first is my friend, Stan Olitz."

Joss extends her little hand, "Pleasure to meet you, Stoltz."

The President smiles, "She has nicknames for all of us. She calls me Prez—-but only she can call me that. Must respect the office, you know."

Stan smiles, patting her on the head, "Well, with all due respect, the President's little girl can call me anything she wants ...as long as her Daddy agrees."

The President has an agenda, "Well, moving along—-I'd like you to meet our second guest. His name is Tito. Traditionally at Thanksgiving, we grant a pardon. And today we're going to pardon Tito."

Joss grabs her daddy's leg, "Please pardon me, too. I don't like turkeys."

The President laughs, "That's okay. I don't either ...try working with them. Try getting something passed through Congress."

The President's wife comes into view, taking Joss by the hand, an already prepared plate of food in the other hand. The President motions for Stoltz to be seated at the banquet table.

The President faces the television cameras, "This time of year, we try to focus on giving thanks—-our greatest thanks to those we should most be thankful for. Foremost on my list are my dad and mom. Most of you would agree with me—-and that's why Thanksgiving has become the busiest time of year for travel. We don't just generate our well-wishing across a computer screen. Nothing beats a real hug. And I've invited my very own parents here, to the White House, for Thanksgiving. They won't be joining us right away though. They've already fixed their plates and are in another room watching the football game with my wife's parents."

The President chuckles, "If my dad's team loses, we won't be able to talk to him for days. So, I plan to introduce my parents to you at halftime. But before we get caught up in all that, or intercepted—-I'm beginning to fumble on my words here—-but, I'd like to thank all the wives and moms. With the football game on, they are most likely our largest audience right now. They are the ones who normally painstakingly prepare these huge delicious Thanksgiving meals."

The President lifts a fork and takes a healthy mouthful. He chews a couple times, "This dressing is delicious. I don't have to ask who made it. Mom makes the best dressing."

The President finishes his mouthful, "I also want to thank my wife for always standing by me, and behind me—-but never in front. Mom taught me to stand—-and what to stand for. I'm always learning new things from my mom. Just yesterday, she'd told me something that I never knew. She told me that she can't stand football. I would have never guessed that. She's always there at dad's side, rooting right along with him. I'd say that along with my little Joss, the three most important women in my life are great examples of what commitment is."

The President lifts a glass to his mouth, taking a drink, "For a couple decades now, it's been tradition for the President to invite one additional guest, outside of the family, whom everyone would agree to be a friend of the nation—-someone we all can be thankful for. I've decided to invite Stoltz because the world peace we've experienced for two and a half years now can be mostly accredited to Stan's commitment towards peace. We owe much thanks to Stan."

The President smiles as he looks over at Stan, "Stan is a good speaker. He could probably do a better job than me, but I can't have that ...I'm the President, and this is my show. Besides, Stan is my guest and I want him to relax and enjoy this Thanksgiving feast."

The cameras span over to Stan, who takes a humongous bite of food, chewing with cheeks bulging, while nodding in affirmation.

The cameras return to the President, "I had Stan's permission to share with you a few really significant moments in his life which he feels were instrumental in giving him a thankful spirit. When Stan was very young, he was the only survivor of a dreadful fire which destroyed his family and home. One of the most memorable moments for Stan was when George Olitz took him in—-later adopting him as his own son. That in itself was perhaps the greatest expression of love, yet for a young boy who had just lost his family, he could not discern between whether it was kindness at its highest level, or actual genuine love. As a young boy, confused by the tragic events of life, he sought after affirmation of that love. One event, he has told me, stands paramount in having taught him of the difference between kindness and love."

The President takes another bite of food, chewing a couple times, "Some food for thought here ...kindness can be friendly or sympathetic. Love, on the other hand, is a deep attachment or devotion, placing a much higher value on the loved one than on yourself."

The President takes a sip of water, "I'm going to show you a clip. It's a reenactment of an incident that happened early in Stan's life." He continues to speak, along with the visuals on the clip, "George had ordered a new Mercedes with On-Star, now standard on all vehicles. Stan told me that at that time, he felt that George loved that Mercedes more than anything else. Then George was a victim of a car-jacking. A young man on a motorcycle had caused an accident, then in his madness, the young man bludgeoned George unconscious."

As the video clip ends, the cameras return to the President, "Now, I ask you, what would you do?"

The President takes another gulp of water, "Personally, I would not know what to do. I do not have the mind of an Olitz. Most of us would agree with the criticalness of precise action in a moment like that. But equally important is the ability to afterwards assimilate all that had taken place. And that's what our George Olitz did. Throughout the years, this incident pulled on Stan's heartstrings in a major way. And it put into motion that which I consider the three most important factors in a productive life. That's why I've included that short clip—-so you can partially see where I'm coming from."

The huge screen provides the brief outline, "The first factor is that we feel secure and provided for. In the loss of Stan's family, George aimed to make Stan feel secure and he made provision for that. The second factor is that we feel loved. This video clip documents an event in Stan's life which was a pivotal point in emotional commitment, which helped convince Stan that he was loved. And the third important factor in our lives is to take that secure feeling and extend the love to others, helping to provide for them, in like fashion as it had been provided for us."

The President leans forward in his chair, yet still remains upright, "As President of the United States, it is my desire and my responsibility to provide those things to our nation. The Office that I hold, along with the members of Congress and all our staff, have not achieved that goal. The Office does not hold your trust in leadership. We have failed to the point that we have little in common with our forefathers—-those who fought to make our nation strong."

The President continues his very serious demeanor, "Since I took office in January of this year, I've not been able to achieve what I had hoped to do. Nor would I be able to achieve it in four years or even eight years, if I were to be re-elected. But I can guarantee you one thing. This is the first time a President has stood before you with this message, and you may ask, what kind of message is this—-from your Commander-in-Chief? It is a sad, but honest message. But it is also a true message. We are a dying nation. Our United States are states without unity. Many of you don't want to hear this, but it is true. And do you know what's also true? It's also true that I still love my country. Tell me, how many of you can still say that? Or how many of you long to say it, but can't?"

The President raises his right hand, "I do not want to be one of many successive Presidents—-who have failed you. I pledge to you, the American people, that I want to rise up to meet the challenge. We are still a mighty nation. We still successfully police the world. And we have a person with us today who has helped bring world peace, where many have deemed it impossible. I am not a proud person. Yes, I am your President, but I'm also still a person. And personally, I see the grave circumstances before us as a nation—-but I also see the person before us who can help overcome seemingly near hopeless circumstances."

The President folds his hands in front of him, "I've invited Stan to join us this Thanksgiving, not only to honor him for all he has done, but because I believe he is not done. Stan has a resolve that resides within him. Stan will not be satisfied until we have peace as a nation, peace within our nation, and peace within ourselves. Stan and I talked about this earlier. As President, I feel that if we cannot have peace within our nation, we cannot have peace within ourselves. But Stan brought it to my attention that it may be the other way around."

The camera pans in for a close-up of the President, "When a loved one passes on, we should assess the value of those things that are passed on. When Stan lost his dad earlier this year, he did not lose the vision his dad left with him. The entire world had shared that same vision while putting their trust in Stan and George. I joined the world in putting my trust in Stan at that time—-and I'm putting my trust in him now. I'm also asking each and every one of you for your trust. I do not want to be the President of a dying nation. The bottom line is, the heart of our nation is failing us and we need some major surgery before we flat-line. I cannot revive our nation on my own. I need the support of all of you."

The President finishes his glass of water, "It has often been said that through the greatest of ideas, the greatest of works, the greatest of accomplishments—-we find achievements by the efforts of those who've had the resolve to survive the most intense pain or the most prolonged suffering. Yet, through the arduous process of enduring, spawns true sacrifice and the birth of new ideas. I cannot think of any more intense pain than that of losing one's entire family. Stan was just a young boy when faced with that tragedy. As we have become a nation in drastic decline, many of you have been forced to face what Stan had to face as a young boy. Families devastated and ripped apart, not by a tragic accident nor a violent act—-but by the tragedy of a nation failing to meet the needs of its own people. We have lost the hope of survival. We all need that glimmer of hope that Stan possesses. Perhaps you can find hope in the one who has gone through what many of you are going through."

The President appears touched by his own words, pauses for a brief moment, takes a deep breath, then proceeds, "I am going to jog your memory just a bit, reviewing a bit of recent history. Most of you remember when our military replaced their dog tags with the *'Chip'*. The *'Chip'* had much varied potential, but our society was not quite ready to accept it. The general public didn't view themselves as a military nation. So, instead, George Olitz convinced some corporate pioneers to develop a watch that had a tracking device. Society embraced the idea for the elderly. And a similar belt was designed for children. But society as a whole did not like the tracking device idea. That did not stop George Olitz. He could not forget that near tragic incident that I showed you on the clip."

The President leans forward in his chair, "Most of you probably didn't know that the evolution of the Olitz watch began as a result of that one dramatic experience. But since society proved not ready to move along with the technological advances of personal security, George instead focused on a design to ease monetary transactions and bookkeeping. With the help of his son, Stan, together they designed a watch with the center dial acting as a scanning device for monetary accounts. The convenience soon proved itself, and we moved with relative ease into a cashless society, as a result of what we all know as the *'Olitz watch'*. But back then, crime was at an all-time low and consumer confidence at an all-time high. You know what happened next. As with all good things, we also have to absorb the bad. As business flourished, crime suffered a temporary loss. But crime is also a business. It would not suffer long. It was sure to find its angry way."

The President now continues very emphatically, "That does not mean that the technological ideas were wrong. I firmly believe that technology can overcome its own small obstacles. I believe the solution has already been provided for us. I believe the solution is Stan. We need someone who is not only capable of seeing the 'big picture'—-but also someone with the dedication and diligence, the self-sacrificial capacity for genius, and the providence to oversee it. And I believe Stan is the man. He has not only the genius to solve, but the resolve and ability to lead. Stan is the best that I know in bridging ideas and bringing people together under those ideas.

That's what our country needs. I believe that is what our country wants. And as I remain President, that is what our country will get."

∗∗∗∗∗∗∗∗∗∗∗

Later that evening, Stan and the President meet in closed quarters. The President assures Stan, "I will give you all the resources you need. But, of course, no one has as many resources as you do. You don't even need my help, really. Yet, what I will give you, is my word. I will not stand in your way. You have my word on that. I have total confidence in you, Stan. I have never met anyone more capable and confident as you, yet, I sense a slight bit of uneasiness. I must ask ...what is it, Stan?"

Stan admits, "It's my fiancée."

Stan clasps both hands behind his neck to relieve some of the tension, "How is it that the entire walled community just—-up and disappears? I do have my theories, but theories based on feelings without facts could lead to diagnosed paranoia. On the other hand, basing everything solely on what we call cold hard facts, can make us a cold hard person—-and it greatly limits our ability to relate as a person."

Stan breathes deeply, "Yes, I have my thoughts and I have my facts, but I also have to realize that insight does not always go hand-in-hand with foresight. Yet still, there is a proverb that states: Where there is no vision, the people perish. And there's definitely something going on in our country. And it cannot be read like a print sheet of crime statistics. I am not going to go public with this, but I will tell you, Mr. President."

∗ ∗ ∗ ∗ ∗ ∗ ∗ ∗ ∗

Stan recalls the lengthy conversation he just recently had with Scottie, who had identified himself as the dad of Murray and Sweeney. It was no secret that Rebekkah had given each of Scottie's two sons a Clipper ship. What was hard to swallow for Scottie was the fact that Sweeney's ship was found in the possession of a local fisherman, docked at Goose Bay in the Newfoundland area. Scottie said Sweeney never did know how to do a real day's work, let alone appreciate a gift.

Scottie had presented the whole sad story of how a dad is not to blame for what his children become. He insisted he'd tried his best, but what is a father to do? Even as a child, Sweeney seemed to resent anyone telling him what to do.

Scottie tried to provide this as some sort of psychological explanation. He said the proper way to bring up a child is to tell them precisely what you want them to do, then stick with it. But Sweeney was a boy who seemed to resent being told what to do. So, naturally, working for Rebekkah just shoved the problem deeper. Scottie offered his bold assessment by stating that when a person is told what to do, they either do it cheerfully, or they have a begrudgin' attitude. And with Rebekkah no longer alive, Scottie felt Sweeney's resentment went AWOL.

Stan recalls how he'd asked the question, "Hadn't Sweeney recently become a Christian?"

But, Scottie had not wanted to discuss that. He felt Sweeney had become a vigilante of sorts, but with no knowledge of what was right or wrong. "Takin' a life into your own hands is not right!"

Stan recalls how he had cited it as merely a common occurrence among newly committed Christians. He'd explained it as the parable of the sower: Some seed falling by the wayside, some upon stony ground, and some among the thorns—-with the thorns, the cares of the world, and the deceitfulness of riches choking you away. But hearing Scottie tell it, you'd be sure to picture it as Sweeney being a thorn in his dad's side. And it'd be difficult to tell who was allowing resentment to rule their life—-a son resenting an overbearing dad, or a dad resenting an independent thinker for a son. Either way, it appeared that both had found enough grief in their cozy little family unit ...whoever's fault it may be. Some people find it cozy playing the 'blame-game'. Scottie had felt he'd endured enough unwarranted punishment in having to raise a son like Sweeney. He didn't want to endure the legacy of being known as his dad.

Scottie's grand summation of the world is that it's always so quick to place blame. But Stan reassures Scottie he will not reveal that Sweeney is the responsible one ...that is, the one responsible for being irresponsible. What Scottie had told him will remain confidential; and Stan promises to deal with it without dragging Scottie's name into all of this.

It's amazing how we can so easily accuse others, claim how shameful it is to do so, yet somehow manage to be one of the greatest offenders. Yes, everyone can be guilty of a bit of ignorance in some area or another in their life. Anyone can be a bit insensitive, while not realizing it. But some seem to excel in these areas. Yet, can we say they don't really know it?

Sweeney is very aware that much of who we are develops through misdirected influences. And the worst can emerge from a group mentality. An angry mob type personality gathered for the crucifixion of Jesus ...and He said, "Father, forgive them, for they know not what they do." Dad wasn't part of a group, and you'd think he'd be aware of what he is doing, so wouldn't he know it? Well, Dad really needs to know Him whose guidance would reveal these things.

Scottie doesn't have many friends ...and those whom he feels he has as friends are not really friends, but are just mutually miserable like he is. Instead of striving for *'better'*, he thrives in *'bitter'*. And somehow he feels obliged to reveal a recent association his son is having with a black man named Angelo. His reasoning is that his son, Sweeney, is by no means a son to be proud of ...but he probably wouldn't have done what he did, if not for this Angelo character.

XLII.

The President again addresses the nation. It is in celebration of the New Year, televised from the White House, "Many of you may feel you've little reason to celebrate. I have promised you a brighter future. But many of you may ask, Mr. President, when will that be? As your President, I feel I owe you an answer. My answer will provide hope and cause to celebrate. My answer is—-this year. The brighter future will come before the close of this year. And at this time, I'd like to turn it over to *'Mr. Hope'*, himself, Stan Olitz."

Stan addresses the nation, "Thank you, Mr. President. Yes, we do share a common vision for a brighter future. I see the idea of world peace moving beyond that of collective cooperation and respect among nations. Lasting peace has to be something of a deeper nature. It has to be more than peace within a nation. We can have equality of peoples and opportunities, yet that in itself does not bring peace. The business that provides the greatest equality of opportunity is the business of crime. Organized crime thrives on opportunity. But peace can only exist when a feeling of security and overall well-being is experienced by every individual."

Stan takes a sip of water, "Peace begins at home and within families, but in our imperfect world, it relies heavily upon a strong commitment to uphold justice. Upholding justice does not limit itself to prosecuting individuals proven to be unjust. It also includes working to make right that which proves to be unjust. So, if crimes are committed, they are crimes committed out of greed, not committed out of desperation. Those who want to do good, should be provided for. My goal is to eliminate crimes of desperation. A line should be drawn between those who resort to crime to get by, and those who use crime to buy resorts. Crime affects our lives on every level. Crime is a threat to individuals, to families, to our states, and to our nation. So much lost revenue is a result of crime.

Drugs suck the very core out of our communities—-not only leaving those communities with countless many nonproductive members, but also leaving just a shell of an individual, forcing so many to lose a vital member of their loving family. Corporate scams rob so many individuals of their investments—-and their future. Malpractice claims and insurance fraud also severely cripple the medical field's affordability, making it extremely difficult for a family to manage health care. But the single largest loss of revenue, categorically, is computer fraud."

The President interjects, "There are many computer geniuses out there, but none come close to your genius, Stan."

It's a relaxed setting at the White House, sort of like a talk show setting. Stan rests his left foot across his right knee, "During the past couple months, I've put my primary effort into devising a network to expose computer fraud. I'm at the point now where I can delegate much of the work."

The President points to Stan, "Any good corporate head knows how to effectively delegate."

Stan smiles, "Yes, we're giving all corporations the necessary resources to continue on with their area of expertise. And we are investing in other corporations that show promise towards new and inventive ideas. The area which I deem of utmost importance is the area of providing for the personal health and safety of each and every human being. And this is the area I am presently giving my primary focus to. We have always aspired to world peace, yet world peace does not automatically bring about peace for you and me. In the past, many nations have predicted that our nation will crumble from within. I am one American who will not just idly stand by and let that happen. My associates and I are working on the availability of a program already tested and proven in our esteemed military, yet they must have availability of resources and at the same time be provided with the tech skills to help minimize the risk of any covert actions disrupting their maneuvers. I believe making this same concept available to the public can all but eliminate crime."

The President challenges, "How do you discern who will use the program for the mutual benefit of all and who would attempt to further their own agenda?"

Stan tries his best not to sound defensive, "As you know, my corporation is on the cutting edge of—-."

The President interrupts with a chuckle, "You are a very humble man, Stan. There is no doubt that you can develop this program. You don't have to convince me. But, for the sake of our viewers, can you explain how you plan to identify those of the criminal element?"

Stan smiles, "I don't have to ...they will identify themselves. They won't step forward to be a part of the program. By their failure to cooperate, they will identify themselves. I believe we are waging a war within our own borders—-and I believe we are losing that war. Any war always seems to be economic in nature. And I believe the same is true for our nation. The very core of our economy is being sucked out by this tidal wave of crime. But I believe that can change—-if we are willing to work together. My plan will not work with partial commitment. For it to be effective, we must all work together."

The President clarifies, "So, what you'd want us to believe is that we need this program?"

Stan laughs, "As you said before, I'm not trying to convince you, but for the benefit of our viewers, yes, I will explain why I believe we need this program. It's not just because we have this extensive network of crime. Suppose we had zero crime in our nation. Through mere mishap and misfortune, we would still need a police department, a fire department, and medical rescue teams. We would still want to be confident that our emergency teams are proficient and expedient in performing their tasks. Likewise, when we've sent soldiers to war, we always hope to account for, locate, and rescue all our casualties."

Stan takes a sip of water, "This plan I'm proposing would benefit us all, whether in time of war or in time of peace. But again, it will only be effective to the degree we work together."

The President summarizes, "So, what you're saying is, we need this program and it will only work if we all work together. Yet, you have already contended that there will be those who don't want to work with us."

Stan barely allows the President to finish, "In a country run by a dictator, the people would be forced to adopt it—-but we are a democracy. In a democracy, the people have a say in the matter. And they get to vote. But once they vote, they are expected to be mature enough to accept that which the majority has voted upon. That is the beauty of democracy. And through the democratic process, it is more easily accepted if it's understood that the majority want it—-more so, than if no one wants it, and it is forced upon them."

The President inquires, "Do you think you can provide the public with a quality product by election time this year?"

Stan smiles with confidence, "I believe the program will be ready by mid-summer."

The President smiles, "So, this coming November we will all vote—-and stand prepared to accept what the majority will decide."

The President gulps his water, "Are there any final thoughts on the matter?"

Stan seems to zone into a more serious frame of mind than he has all evening, "As I've already said, there are those who prosper at the wrongs of the throngs of society, capitalizing on our social ills. There's been a resurgence of organized crime. Sadly enough, most of us have come to accept this. Well, I cannot accept it. Those who, through the victimization of others, have prospered greatly, will no longer prosper. Some of you may think I'm going a bit overboard with all of this, but let me share something with you. I was not going to mention it, but you have the right to know. It's not something that just affects me. We are in this together. It affects us all. There are groups out there who are trying to erode our society, the very fiber of that which holds us together. And to a certain extent it has been working. During this telecast, if I've appeared defensive ...it's because I am. Can you hear commitment in the tone of my voice? I want everyone to know, I will not be defeated. I will fight for you—-the people—-even harder now."

The President voices support, "I agree ...it's time you American people know."

Stan takes a deep breath, "One of these groups is holding my fiancée hostage. And they are doing it under the guise of religion. Since her disappearance, I've been sending a million dollars, each day—-to guarantee her survival. You may ask, wouldn't the computer genius know who is extorting money from him? Yes, I quickly traced the account I was told to send the money to. I know who is behind it. But, I don't know where they are keeping my fiancée. That has become my own private torment. I imagine her crying out to me, desperately praying for me to come to her rescue. But, I can't! I don't know where she is. I seldom get more than an hour or two of sleep each night, waking up from my fitful sleep, perspiring heavily. I return to my computer, searching for a clue that perhaps they've left behind. So, you see, this is the ultimate reason I am driven to develop this program—-so this will never happen again, to anyone!"

Stan wipes the perspiration from his forehead, "I believe this program is a good program. And I would have worked on this program anyway, but the intensity that I bring to the program, I have to admit, is because of what happened to my fiancée. It is my sincere hope that each of you could be spared an event like this ever happening to any of you. We should be able to wake up each morning and look upon the day with a bright outlook. I want each person's morning to be bright. That is why I've decided to call this project, *Morning-Star.* Actually, George and I had been working out details towards this end, for years. We've always believed that the idea behind a National I.D. was a good one. The torment of what I've suffered over the kidnapping of my finance' could have been avoided. But the program I'm developing goes way beyond that. There are many tragedies that can be avoided. Crime visits our many homes in a violent fashion daily. There is no time more pressing!"

XLIII.

For half a dozen months, Stan rarely sleeps more than a couple hours each night. Then on June 30th, Stan sleeps for eighteen hours. On July 1st, Stan is to meet with the twelve most loyal corporate heads of the conglomerate—-Star Corporation. The nation is about to celebrate Independence Day, but Stan wants to check to see if they all are still on the same page, after the great merger. Stan wants to see if anyone has any independent thoughts. For it to work, they have to all stand together.

The one who helped the most with heading up the project, the most senior member, stands, "I feel I'm not only speaking for myself, but for the entire group. I like being a light unto you, per se. I like the responsibility of representing you. I don't desire the freedoms inherent in separate corporations. I only desire to proudly represent you the best way I can. You've given us freedoms to everything there is within the new conglomerate. I am grateful for that. I've always looked forward to serving you. I'm happy and content with the corporate arrangement. Everything began with you. You built it up. We could never manage the corporation as you have. None of us have ever invested anything in the corporation, but we drink from the wells of prosperity. You've proven how much you care. How could we ever trust anyone else to handle the corporation as you have? You are the corporation! How can we not accept that? Our loyalty is to you—-to the corporation. I am who I am because of you. All my praise and thanks go out to you."

The group stands. They all applaud. There is nothing more anyone can say. They all stand in agreement.

Stan smiles. It touches his innermost pride, "It is a pleasure to work with the likes of men such as you. It is a pleasure to be the recipient of such loyalty and gratitude."

****

In the following months, the economy makes a small recovery, investing in the faith of Stan. It is a fair autumn. There is a bit of uneasiness, but mostly guarded optimism. They are eager for Stan's plan. They have faith in Stan. They are just uncertain how they can trust each other.

****

It is less than a month before the election. Then, without warning, all at once—-it happens! After 42 months of world peace, the entire world falls into chaos.

The world will never forget it. Etched into everyone's minds, it appears across computer screens—-across the world. The man sits cross-legged. He has a covering upon his head. His eyes are concealed behind tinted glasses. His face is covered by a long scraggly grey beard.

He speaks English—-good English. The obvious accent is unrecognizable, probably intentionally. He is an educated man. His message is clear, "In forty-five minutes, the Freedom Tower in New York City will be destroyed. That should get your attention! Go ahead, get to it! Do what you are trained to do! I will wait for you to complete your response ...then I have more important things to discuss with you."

Many of the heroes of September 11th, 2001 are still alive. Only a few are still employed in the same capacity, but those few have provided the highest degree of leadership. And today, they will lead again. The rescue teams spring into action. The Freedom Tower must be evacuated at once! There is no time to lose! Every person must be accounted for.

The beauty of everyone working together for one common purpose, and willing to give their lives to save others—-proves to be successful. The Freedom Tower blows up—-but remarkably, no one is inside. No one is injured.

The old grey bearded man waits on the screen. At the fifty minute mark, the Freedom Tower is totally leveled. The bearded man speaks, "Good job! You have done well. Now you realize why you are a 'chosen people'. No one else in the world springs into action like you do. Good job! You have proven worthy of my next task. You have self-appointed yourself as the watchdogs of the world. You carry the humanitarian banner. But now, you also carry the war banner. Someone has now declared war on the world. You don't know who it is—-you don't know who I am. Don't try to find me. You won't be able to."

****

Stan has already tried to track the computer message. He sits in front of his screen, as others across the nation sit in front of theirs. But it is more haunting for Stan. Stan doesn't know who the bearded man is, but he knows the bearded man's words are directed at him.

The bearded man continues, "Stan, I'm sure you've already discovered this is a timed message. I am nowhere near the location where this message was entered. Enough about me, how are you doing? Don't lose your focus now. I have confidence in the people of your country. I know they are capable of great things. I was confident the Freedom Tower would be successfully evacuated. I am also confident that you, Stan, will successfully help lead your nation. Your people are accustomed to carrying the banner of peace, not of war. Other nations of the world look to you for guidance during times of peace and during times of war. These other nations are being hit hard by biological agents. They need your help! Don't let them down—-they're counting on you. Carry on the peace, Stan, the war will take its own course. Don't try to fight a war you don't even understand. Preserve the peace. No ruler, whether it be King or Queen, Caliph or Chief, Czar or Zealot, President, Pontiff, or Potiphar—-has ever been able to rally the people, to rally nations, as you have. Preserve the peace, Stan."

Stan checks all his international communications. Schools, universities, and hospitals around the world are reporting the spread of biological agents reaching epidemic proportions.

Not that long after George Olitz had passed away, corporate leadership, along with all that power, had transferred over to Stan. And just recently Stan had bought two of the largest drug companies, to merge with the largest, which he already owned. Stan contacts the company to increase the production of Cipro. The news media had just reported confirmation of Anthrax, spreading throughout Central and South America.

The next wave of reports come from South and Southeast Asia, including the islands of Indonesia. The rapid spread of smallpox raises havoc in that area of the world. Then a double-whammy, when SARDS is identified in several heavily populated areas.

Next, Africa reports in. "So far, we've not yet identified what is suddenly plaguing our most populated areas, but our news sources say our medical experts have an idea."

Stan notifies them that his company will send someone out there to verify it. And they will bring with them the expected drug so they can begin treating it—-if their guess is correct.

The worst reports are those coming in from New Zealand, Australia, the Soviet Republic, and throughout all of Europe. The early accounts are scattered and confusing, but the experts soon verify it as the most deadly version of Missionary Dysentery, or as some call it, Island Sickness ...which had previously been isolated on the islands of Indonesia, and had only been treated successfully on Missionary Island.

When Stephen Razohn had come down with Missionary Dysentery, they had begun experimenting with new treatments for it on Missionary Island. But even before that, George had tried for years to work with Missionary Island. The problem was Rebekkah's son, Stephen Tressel. Stephen had too many reservations about drug companies. He would not work with George. He said that the disease was limited to the islands of Indonesia, and they were more than adequately taking care of it within their hospital. But now, Stan is confident that he can convince Stephen otherwise. With such a horrific outbreak of epidemic proportions, how can he be denied?

Stan tries to get in touch with Missionary Island, but he can't reach anyone. He keeps trying with no success. So finally, in a fit of frustration, he decides to fly to Missionary Island.

On the flight there, Stan reaches the President. The President is pleased to hear of the drug production that Stan has already stepped up. The President asks, "Do you have any idea who this grey bearded man is? Or why he is focusing so directly on you?"

Stan hesitates, "No, I wish I had some idea who this character is. He may be tied to the ones who kidnapped my fiancée. That's why I'm not sending someone else on this trip. If there is a connection, I want to deal with this character myself. The only reason I can see why he's focusing on me, is to rattle me into reacting irrationally. Everyone knows the unity I've helped establish from nation to nation. He's wrong if he thinks he can disrupt that unity. Some changes will have to be made, but we will continue our resolve. In the face of adversity, we will only get stronger."

As they land on Missionary Island, Stan immediately gets a lump in his throat. He swallows hard. There is a Clipper ship sitting in the harbor. But no sign of what happened here.

There is absolutely no sign of anyone—-anywhere. Not a single person is on the island.

Stan gets a very disturbing feeling. He had taken a small army with him, as a precautionary measure. He wanted protection in case something went wrong. But no army could protect him from an invisible war—-a war of the mind.

Stan's mood picks up a bit when a couple of his soldiers find a mammoth stockpile of the raw material used to combat Missionary Dysentery. It wouldn't take long to mass produce the drug, and make it available to the masses.

XLIV.

Just days before the election, the President and Stan coordinate their steps. Though they will be in different parts of the globe, both will be televised. The President leaves Mexico City, arriving in Columbia. Stan has already visited Paris, Rome, and Baghdad. He is in flight to Israel, when he tunes in to the President.

The President is about to broadcast his humanitarian relief effort to hospitals in Columbia, when he gets a report that hospitals and schools throughout the United States are being targeted with biological attacks.

The President addresses the nations, "I believe we have had great success here and throughout the globe. We've been able to stem this wave of terrorism. Do we truly believe this will be the end?—-No. We should all be on high alert, and be continually prepared to rally to the cause of helping our dear neighbors. We have stood ready, not knowing where they will attack next. All along, we expected this. We never thought we'd be exempt. I've just been given a report that they've targeted hospitals and schools back in the U.S.—-so, I'm convinced they will stop at nothing. But we will not stop either. I've already called for an immediate evacuation of all schools and hospitals. We are going to transfer all medical operations to mobile units and also set up stationary operations in our local churches. I am calling upon all the local churches in cities throughout the nation to not only reach out to provide availability of their buildings, but also to provide around the clock prayer vigils. And everyone needs to get vaccinated."

The President hesitates, as if to reflect, "I've learned a valuable lesson in the past few days. We've tried to combat terrorism and be the protector of the earth, but we alone can *never* do it. And I don't mean *we*, as the United States, but *we*, as nations of the earth, can no longer do it. We cannot do it together as we resolved to do it. We cannot establish a lasting world peace. We need to pray to the Essence, to guide us in the steps we must take. Perhaps the steps you are to take are the steps to the voting booth. We've also transferred those to the local churches. That's what we, in the U.S., will be doing tomorrow. Perhaps every nation throughout the earth will gather their own people together, and strive to find similar solutions—-perhaps the same solution. We have reached out to you in a time of real need. This is not a fleeting moment of compassion, affirming ourselves. We have demonstrated a commitment and are prepared to stand with you."

"This is Jan Lather, reporting to you with the President, from Columbia. Now we will take you to the Middle East, where Stan Olitz is standing by."

Stan is aboard a flying platform that has landed on a small plateau in a barren area, surrounded down below by a rather large gathering of people wrapped in cloths, dirty and torn. To many, it is a rather hideous sight, but to Stan it is an opportunity. This is being taped for live coverage. The camera spans to a crudely constructed sign below. It reads: Leper Colony.

Stan is helping distribute food and basic medical supplies, including bandages and ointments. This is Stan's backdrop, as he is being televised, "It is difficult enough dealing with all that happens naturally, without terrorism. We need to help each other endure through the natural disasters, not create more for ourselves by wreaking havoc on each other."

The camera focuses in on this picture of frantic desperation, as the supplies are being received within the colony. They tear open the supply bundles for temporary inspection with an outright display of mistrust. It is an intense moment, very newsworthy and one that tugs at the heartstrings.

As they complete the shoot and prepare to pack up and leave, Stan places a call to the President. The President is eager to hear from Stan, "How is your trip going, Stan?"

Stan stares once again towards the sickly crowd below, hidden beneath their own obvious hideousness, clothes draped over their heads, "We're just about to leave this colony in Israel. We just heard about it and I thought it would be great for the American people to see. This is really disturbing. I can't believe areas allow themselves to regress, to isolate themselves from the technologies and modern medicines of the world. How they choose to live like this, I will never understand. It's been hundreds of years, you'd think no one would have to live like this. It reminds me of the movie, 'Ben-Hur'. That used to be one of my favorite movies."

The President recalls, "Wasn't that the very same guy who used to represent the National Rifle Association?"

Stan affirms, "Yes, he first became popular by doing all those movies about Bible characters."

The President adds, "That's right—-I remember him now. Ben-Hur was about that Jesus character, wasn't it?"

Stan affirms, "That's the one. It used to be a classic."

The President is curious, "So, that was one of your childhood favorites, huh? Did you used to believe in that Bible stuff?"

Stan hesitates, "Well, my dad, George, used to pretend to believe in it. So I just sort of went through the motions with him."

The President sighs, "Well, I'm ready to go through the motions of sleep. I'm going to request not to be disturbed. There will be plenty to take care of when we get back home. See you back in the States."

Stan adds, "Don't forget to vote tomorrow, Mr. President."

****

As the flying platform takes off, Stan takes one last aerial view of the long line of lepers, carrying supplies across a rocky terrain and through a narrow passageway cut between a face of steep rock. A small child is lagging behind, barely able to carry the load.

Stan hopes to carry the image that the world can still be provided for. This will do well to show the world who to put their trust in ...and Stan will do his best to make sure no one has to live like this.

In retrospect, Stan realizes that he has been well-provided for. He is very thankful for the corporate power that George has left him. He can't imagine having to live any other way, let alone living like this colony of lepers. They have no idea what comforts life can provide.

As the flying platform travels out-of-view to a location where Stan's jet awaits, an older person waits for the small child at the end of the line. The older person also carries a bundle, yet politely looks back to see how the child is managing.

Encouraging speech travels from the woman to the small child, "Many times people think we are ignorant because we choose not to live like others. But we know what life is about if we understand our inheritance."

The small child asks, "What is ignorant?"

The Mom laughs, "Most children your age would rather ask what inheritance is."

The child stops, drops his bundle and pulls back his head covering, catching a slight breeze, revealing a smile, "I know what inheritance is."

The Mom stops and drops her bundle also, explaining, "Well, ignorant means having lack of knowledge in a particular area. You can be ignorant in one area, yet have much knowledge in another.

Ignorance is not necessarily a bad thing. It can be a help to be ignorant to the ways of the world. But sadly, the ways of the world are mostly ignorant to the wonderful inheritance that could be theirs—-through Jesus."

The small boy scratches the top of his head, "I know about Jesus, but I think I'm still ignorant about ignorant."

The small boy picks up his bundle again. A much older boy comes into view, carrying a much heavier load, "Let me take your burden, little brother. Seems like you already have a heavy load to carry—-on your mind."

The older brother grabs his young brother's bundle, "I don't really understand it either, Mom. Isn't it sometimes good to have knowledge of the ways of the world?"

The Mom wants to test the older son's understanding, "How do you mean?"

The older son explains, "Well, if you know of something bad, then maybe you can help stop the bad thing."

The Mom answers simply, "That is true."

The younger son looks up to Mom in confusion, "Then why didn't we stop the bad things from happening?"

The Mom attempts to talk on both of their levels, "It's like the story book about the 'bully'. He needs extra special prayer because as bad as he seems, what he really needs is to take to heart the story of Jesus. But if the bully begins doing some really bad things, we try to stop it. We've created a sort of dilemma here. Are we to say that prayer alone isn't enough? In some circumstances it seems we need to try to put action to our prayer."

The older son asks, "How do we know when to wait for an answer to prayer and when to take action?"

The Mom sighs, "Yes, that's a difficult one. It's kind of like the serenity prayer: To change the things we can, to accept that which we cannot change, and the wisdom to know the difference. But we can always pray."

She takes another deep breath, "The sad part is when someone like your younger brother has to witness all this. It is so tragic when young children have to witness all these horrors of war, and the oppression it brings. And it is usually the result of wealth and the governments that cater to it. Children who grow up with war and oppression, often eventually adopt the anger, hate, and ideals of those around them. They don't often learn the pathway to peace, but instead travel the nightmarish path of their past experiences and upbringing."

The Mom pats her youngest son on the top of his head and ruffles up his already ruffled hair, "You give your precious mind a little rest, I'm going to test your older brother's thinking."

The older son laughs, "Remember, I'm not supposed to look at it as a test. I'm supposed to welcome the opportunity for more creative thinking."

The Mom laughs too, "Sorry, you're right. Let me encourage you along. You're a well-educated young man, I ask you, what business has grossed the second largest amount of income last year?"

The son hesitates, then answers, "The drug business ...first is cybercrime?"

The Mom clarifies, "Correct. And by that, you mean the transfer of illegal drugs."

The son politely responds, "Yes, that's what I meant."

The Mom carries it further, "So, the two top businesses in the nation we've just fled ...are actually illegal businesses, which makes it terribly nonproductive for a nation's health and economy. Yet there are legal businesses which are all too similar to that—-selling out to other nations whose governments' primary concern is not the welfare of their people. It can be said that the way those people are treated is inhumane, actually criminal—-and that would lead one to believe that any nation associated economically with those nations are one in the same—-as they are a party to it."

He is confused, "Why did we leave our country? Why didn't we just stay and fight for what we believe in?"

She is pleased to have her son's undivided attention, "I don't believe we abandoned our country ...they abandoned us. But, here's my question to you: If your neighbor was one of the biggest drug dealers and you had word that a huge drug deal was going to take place next door, would you report it?"

The son adjusts the bundle on his shoulder, standing more upright, "Well, yes!"

The Mom adds, "But you'd hope that the authorities wouldn't just stroll next door and say that they received word that the big drug transaction is going to happen tomorrow ...and ask them if it is true. You would hope they would stake it out, and catch them without revealing the source of who had tipped them off."

The older son gives feedback to his understanding, "If they questioned them the day before, then I'd say the drug drop would not take place. And I would probably be a target for having reported it."

The younger son had not given his ears a rest. The small boy tries to sound not so small, "But wouldn't you feel good about telling?"

The Mom explains, "It's important how and when you tell. If you don't go about it wisely, then they may just find another way. And the other way may be worse."

* * * ** * * *

They slowly pass through the narrow passageway through the steep canyon walls. Within the huge rock face is the entrance to a cave. There is a small light ahead.

Mom sheds her outer garment of rags, letting the hem down on her clean white linen. Her sons do the same, as do the entire group.

Mom turns to her sons, smiling, "Likewise, this mayhem would have found another way. The stakes are so very high, the damage would've still been done. Trying to stop him now will perhaps only make matters worse. But on the other hand, what could be worse than the deception the world now faces?"

The small boy doesn't ask about the steaks costing so much. He feels content to hold onto the hem of his Mom's clean garment as they walk towards the light, growing brighter with each step. The Mom places her bundle down within the well-lit room.

The older son drops both of his bundles beside a pile of soiled and tattered outer garments. They gather around with the others. The bright lights of the cameras center in on a bearded person sitting cross-legged on the floor as they create one more segment for the world to see.

As one of the most negative images of recent times, the bearded person speaks again, "This is the very last time I will make an appearance. I will share with you the most devastating bit of news yet. And don't go away ...I will also reveal to you who I am."

XLV.

This day following the big election, the President and Stan join together standing hand-in-hand, celebrating the election results. With hands raised upward, they step forward.

Stan then takes a step back as the President approaches the podium alone, "The threat of terrorism is ever increasing, but America will not be defeated. Each and every American that went to the polls yesterday, demonstrated their resolve to fight for our rights as Americans. And that was the first step—-a very crucial step. The second and third steps are what I consider critical to our survival. The most urgent is to preserve our food and drinking water. We are asking everyone to access our food supply centers for their drinking water. Also treated as an emergency, we are putting all our effort into getting our hospitals running, without threat of terrorism. Next comes the reason why you voted. I know each and every one of you don't want to live like this forever. And that's why you voted to accept the plan Stan has promised you. My part is to help ease the facilitation of the plan. I am reinstituting the draft. All eighteen and nineteen-year-olds must report. I am asking your sons and daughters to help. Some will be needed overseas to help combat this sudden terrorist threat that we have identified at several key locations across the globe. But more will be needed right here in our own nation to help set up Stan's computerized program at all food centers and hospitals, both of which will be heavily guarded. This program will involve only one simple insert. But with that insert you will insert the most technologically advanced security system of all time. There is nothing you can do that is more secure for you and your loved ones than this system. And it will guarantee we will never have to go through this again. It is a pathway to restoring unto you that which you once had—-that which you deserve—-as Americans."

At the end of the President's brief televised message, something remarkable happens—-something rather shocking! All over the computer screens, the old grey bearded terrorist—-as he is known by—-sits cross-legged, giving a different sort of message, "I am not a terrorist. I merely intercepted the information and tried to warn you of what may happen. Now it's your turn to decide whether you believe me. When faced with fear, you don't know who to trust, having long since abandoned the One you should've trusted. It didn't just happen overnight; it's been a long time coming. Have you accepted the life you now have because it prospers you? Is it a life of quiet comfort, steeped up with compromise ...compromising the very foundations of what you once claimed to believe in? Do you want to hear this? Are you willing to admit you could have been led astray? You must decide! Do you want to face the truth? Do you want to face me?"

The veil is removed, per se. The old grey tattered beard is ripped off. The head covering is removed, revealing long silky black hair. Then the tinted glasses come off. They are not the cold, hard eyes of a terrorist. They are soft eyes, filled with compassion ...the eyes of Lisa Stone.

Lisa continues to talk, "You must decide. But it's not a fair decision unless you have all of the facts. And I know you want to listen to Stan—-because you are scared and he's promising to make it better for you. But do you know, Stan was scared once too? He was just a young innocent child when faced with the cruel fact that his family had been lost in a fire. But he had someone promising to make it better for him. That someone was George Olitz. George had always strived for a better life for himself. For George, better meant more—-more money. But don't take my word for it. I'm through here, for now. I'll let someone else clear up that part of the deception."

Leah Razohn appears across the computer screen, "Stan, I shed my tears when I learned of the deception. I still love you, Stan. Love can be a confusing thing. You had two people save your life, Stan ...Fernye and George. They both showed great acts of love ...but, both were very different people, and it seems you and I are too. The ultimate horror is love that deceives—-because that is not love at all. I admit, it took me a while to get over it, but we don't drink from the same cup, Stan. And this is what each of us must decide for ourselves: From what cup do we drink? What cup do we want to reach for when we are thirsty? What fills us up?"

Leah reaches out her hand and pulls Shannon into view, "It's not important that the nation and the world see we've taken separate paths. It's important that everyone knows what those paths are. What is important is that everyone sees the truth, so they can choose to embrace it. Clever the way you made up that story about paying that exorbitant *ransom* for me ....a million dollars per day to keep me, your fiancée, alive. I don't want that lie to be kept alive. The message I'd like everyone to hear is how Jesus truly paid the *ransom* for our sins. Crucified for our sins ...and desiring for sin not to rule us. Don't let it rule you, Stan."

Sweeney is the next to speak across the screen, "Dad, you will now join the rest of the nation, in viewing a significant piece of evidence. There are only three copies of the expanded version. I have one copy, Lisa Stone has a copy, and the final copy was sent to Stan. The rest of the world saw the more limited version of Rebekkah Lessert's last will and testament. We will now all see what Stan had already seen back then. Dad, I want you to see it because I love you. I want you to see what any of us may have become ...if we'd had the means to achieve it."

The tape of Rebekkah is presented across the computer screen, "You've all had the opportunity to see my first version of my last will and testament. Now, I'd like you to view another version. The last time I talked with you, I merely explained my wish to maintain the status quo. That will not change. But now, I will further detail the 'why' aspect of my decision. George, oh, George, I know you are deteriorating quickly. You probably won't even understand. Alzheimer's disease is such a sad thing. I send my sympathy to you, Stan. And since George's condition is such as it is, I guess I am really leaving this message to you, Stan. Most of you have always seen George as a good, long-time friend. To many of you, it will seem just like that. I've tortured myself many times over wondering why I continue to struggle, and having to face the fact that perhaps I've done much of it to myself. But I've found out that I was not the only one bent on seeking out my torment. It is rather frightening to think that the kindness George has shown me over the years has been for the purpose of manipulation. How many of his relationships have been based on manipulation, deceitfulness, or abusiveness? For a long time now, George has been a sick man. Now, he is a dying man, but he's been a sick man for most of his life. Finding this out did not make my life any more complete. No satisfaction came to me through these revelations. I would have felt fulfilled and satisfied without ever having knowledge of what was recently revealed to me. Though some things are not for our personal well-being, they may be for the benefit of others. What it did for me was not for my benefit. What it did for me was make me angry."

Rebekkah does not look angry now, but she looks tired, and her voice reflects that, "All my years, I fought for what I believed in. Much of that time I spent in anger. I felt vengeful and struggled with what areas of my life I let that anger funnel into. Until I just recently discovered the real George Olitz. Suddenly, vengeance had a name. But just like so many things, it cannot exist past a person's lifetime unless the banner is carried by others to follow. When you convinced those nations in the Middle East to establish peace, Stan, you told them to teach their children to forgive ...to bring about change in their lives. Now it's your turn to do that very thing yourself, Stan. You can stop the madness that George for years worked to create. I didn't even suspect that large sums of money were being subverted to offshore hedge fund accounts. Sort of ironic ...George was using a bank in Bermuda, and my money was disappearing there. But when one microscopic piece of information came my way, it was one piece in a very disturbing puzzle."

*** * * * ***

The President had so quickly entered his private quarters with Stan for a celebratory dinner, he had not seen any of what was televised just after his speech. And he had given strict orders that they were not to be disturbed.

As an Aide to the President tries to get clearance to enter that dinner, the rest of the nation continues to watch their computer screens as Rebekkah's taped message continues, "It wasn't difficult at that point to piece the puzzle together. George used people he felt he could have control over. Why a person is that way, I don't know—-or maybe I do. At times I felt like my whole life was out-of-control, so I attempted to control it. I disregarded God's wisdom by attempting to do what I felt God should be doing. George, on the other hand, did things that you would think no respectful God-fearing man would do. I'm thankful that God did not allow my anger to reach that point in my life. There are certain things George did that we will never know about. Nor do we need to know about them. There are certain secrets that many of us take to the grave with us. Only God knows about those things."

XLVI.

Yes, only God knows how tightly woven are the combined secrets of the multitude. It is all called unconfessed sin. And for those who refuse to acknowledge it, it grows undetected for the most part. When it does rear its ugly head, much of the time it is greeted with denial and plain old 'blame-shifting'. Sin thrives when life is not God-centered. Now there is a big difference between what may be considered *'good'*-centered and God-centered. There are many good men in the world. And it appears most everyone considers Stan one of the *'good men'*. Like many highly esteemed people, he had to overcome a huge tragedy in his life ...but, most would say that Stan's character developed along with an appreciation of George's commitment to him, offering him good guidance and direction. Many would also say that was the primary factor in developing the depth of character that most everyone appreciated in Stan.

Whether it was Stan's character helping him to overcome the tragedy, or the tragedy now aiding Stan in developing his depth of character—-either way, there was no one more highly esteemed than Stan.

Along with George's guidance, there seemed to be an overall striving within Stan towards the *'good'* of all men. George guided Stan into successfully overcoming tragedy, and George believed an entire nation could also benefit this way. George believed a nation could become strong through being tested, and overcoming hardship and tragedy ...history has proven it. But George also believed that tragedy was often necessary, and strength of character couldn't be achieved without it. He might even consider helping it along, for the greater *'good'* of mankind ...or at least for *his* greater *'good'*. And everyone else will have to experience the hardship and tragedy, not him.

This is what he taught Stan, along with always maintaining the *image* ...and not a person could be found that did not imagine that Stan was a *'good'* man. It was all Stan was taught, and it was all he knew ...so, quite naturally, he also believed in the concept.

But what did George believe? What was George taught in his youth while *his* character was developing?

George was taught that if something goes wrong, you cover it up. But that did not mean—-covered with love and forgiveness. No, it was to be covered by lies.

George was taught that lies were sometimes also for the benefit of society ...and in those cases, it wasn't even considered a lie.

What was this special attention that George had always thrived for? The family did not really want to give George that special attention. It was much easier to just attend to the lies ...and see to it that they distance themselves from him and his peculiar ways. But early on, it was quite difficult to achieve this.

Both of George's parents were business-centered. In his early teens, George was encouraged to persist with his studies. He was a bright boy and was expected to follow in the footsteps of his parents. Early on, they were grooming him for the business world. But no one was stressing family values, a sense of morality, nor any mention of God.

Without God, there is no standard. Soon any sense of morality changes. By the time God enters in, the standard has been so lost that it would take a real commitment and desire to follow Jesus to gain back what was lost.

But George accepted in name only. And all the teaching merely stressed the many aspects of God's love, not God's righteousness. So George held a standard different from God's true standard. He had no trouble holding others to a standard, but the standard for himself hid behind a mask of denial—-further masking his own guilt.

Where did it all start? Was it the 'training up a child in the way he should go' ...grooming him for the business world? Or was it the total lack of interest in George as a person? Or more accurately perhaps, was it the total disregard for the Person of God?

When George was old enough to know better, his aunt and uncle would frequently take their ten year-old daughter, Callula, in public with them. People would comment on how attractive she was. Not cute, or even pretty, but attractive. They would comment on how she could possibly be a model some day. But the moment Callula would begin talking, you could tell she would never become a model. The doctor's diagnosis was ...severe mental retardation.

The Olitz family was a proud family. They had stopped taking Callula out in public, so the only time she could be around other people was during family gatherings. During these gatherings the adults would all talk business. And the youth would talk about ...whatever the youth would talk about.

George's cousin liked him. She was content to sit quietly and listen while George did the talking. But sometimes neither one would talk. And George showed Callula things she had never before seen.

With her mental retardation, Callula was just like a child—-a much younger child. She would share the excitement of new things, but only with George. He'd told her it was their own private secret ...and no one would know because they were all quite busy with their business.

The now annual gatherings seemed so far away for Callula. She had a difficult time keeping the secret private. But she knew that she didn't want to share it with anyone in the family.

When she was 13 years old, she began exploring with the boy down the street. He was caught and sent to youth prison. Callula was sent to a mental institution. There they found out she was pregnant. To avoid public criticism, and a media blitz of attention, they quietly had her give birth to her baby girl.

Both of Callula's parents continued to work, and hired a nanny to take care of the child, named Khaki Mae. Callula never did well around babies, so it wasn't until Khaki Mae's 5th birthday that they decided to have Callula rejoin the family gathering. Everyone was talking business again. The get-together seemed to go well enough ...until a few months later, when the mental institution informed the Olitz family that Callula was pregnant again.

They asked if the family had any insight into that. The Olitz family incited panic within the entire facility, assuming one of the staff was the guilty party. They threatened to sue and even hired a private investigator to try to prove the criminal offense. But the guilty party happened to come from—-Khaki Mae's birthday party. The blood type happened to match 22-year-old George.

The family was certain to keep this silent. They were a proud family. They would handle this within the family. And since George had committed the offense, it was George's parents who hired a nanny to take care of the baby boy.

To control George was an entirely separate manner. Everything wasn't on the up and up with the Olitz businesses. But, to conduct business, they couldn't afford to have a liability such as George ...so he was sent packing. There was an associate who had a similar problem with their son ...and had taken shockingly drastic measures with their teenager. George's parents decided to use scare tactics with their own son ...even though he was already a young adult. They didn't know much about the secret and internal effect it had upon their associate's son ...they just saw the life lesson of what they saw as a successful doctor, who they felt had turned his life around.

But, scare tactics often don't work ...and can make matters even worse, bringing about an opposite desired effect. The potential problems could, in fact, double. Well, with the renegade doctor and George having made an acquaintance ...it more than doubled. The doctor and George both just learned the worst from each other ...and any bad experiences they had, they just inflicted that same pain or worse upon others.

For the Olitz family, it was rather convenient not having George around. The nanny not only took care of the baby boy, she also cleaned and cooked for the whole family. This worked out quite well for several years, up until Larry's First Communion at the Catholic Church. They invited Callula for the event, and that proved to be a mistake. Larry didn't seem the same after that. Of course, it was not an error in judgment on their part. They blamed it instead on the nanny. The nanny was readily fired, and they looked for alternative family options for Larry.

A well-meaning young couple from church, Mr. and Mrs. Leper, who couldn't have children of their own, were interested in the young boy. They felt foster care was the answer. Larry even took on their last name.

Meanwhile, George is very familiar with the renegade doctor's methods. George witnesses the extent of what people will go through when they are truly desperate. One particular client peaks his interest. The Tressels have much power and influence, but when power equates to money, the hard lesson is that money can't buy everything. Yet, potential promises can still drain much power ...through deliberate and well-calculated deceit. George seizes the moment with an unexpected turn ...turning Richard's and his parent's death into a triumph of opportunistic circumstances.

George then exposes the Doctor, acting as a savior, while rescuing Richard's wife. The Doctor splits before the authorities can catch up with him. Sarah is grateful, and befriends George as a lifetime friend. Unaware that George is fueling her every fear, she takes his advice and changes her name to Rebekkah. They keep in close contact from that moment on. But the contact is at George's convenience ...and he secretly and conveniently often travels back to his birthplace, where he birthed most of his trouble.

Meanwhile, the young couple from church that had taken Larry were well-meaning, but not well-adjusted. Soon the couple admits that they can no longer handle the boy. The Olitz family does not waste time finding Larry a well-suited group home. It was not well-monitored though. That suited Larry fine, until the unwanted visitor came. Though Larry did not welcome the visitor, the group home found him more than welcome. This individual and his family made large donations to the group home as charitable tax write-offs.

George was allowed to tour the group home to observe what programs the donations provided. But no one monitored what fearful programs George was providing during his every visit. Eventually, George's aunt and uncle tire of caring for Khaki Mae, sending her to that same group home. Strangely, she is housed with her brother—-a brother she has no knowledge of—-who, aside from those annual gatherings, is a stranger to her. Khaki Mae can't escape the torment of George's visits, but she never loses sight of her goal. One day she will become a nurse—-and help people. At least that is her dream.

George convinces himself that everything is under control. He typifies many a generation after generation of people who think nothing of shirking obvious responsibility, with little or no acknowledgement of possible consequences associated with such behaviors. The truth is that George had arranged the disappearance of the Doctor he'd pretended to expose. The Doctor then practices in Europe under a new name, until George calls on him to return.

The Doctor's new assignment is to work on the experimental 4th floor of a mental institution where Rebekkah's son is being held. Nowhere on earth can a Doctor make this kind of money.

And how convenient, that Khaki Mae works at that same facility, fulfilling her goal of becoming a nurse.

George had made certain she got the job ...at the same hospital where her brother was a patient. George was very satisfied with himself, having everyone so neatly under his control, placing all his eggs in one basket, most of them cracked—-and Crazy Larry, occasionally fried.

George doesn't foresee the trouble his son is about to create, nor does he know precisely what Larry knows, but he knows Larry is creating too much difficulty.

When Rebekkah's son escapes, the Doctor then escapes back to Europe, assuming another new name. George sweats this one out, but then begins to feel good about himself. He feels he's off the hook again, and begins to feel he can get away with just about anything. There is no possible trace to him—-or if there is one, he has no knowledge of it.

XLVII.

Rebekkah's stark presentation continues, marking evidence she'd uncovered, "I had no trace of the Doctor who had kept my son on that dreaded 4th floor. But I did have availability of certain information concerning the trace amounts of the drug in my son's system. And it was the same drug used on me, to slow my recovery after my daughter was born. Yes, I, Rebekkah Lessert, am Sarah Tressel. And I am now sending a copy of my book, *'So Loved'*, to my son as an explanation. It may not be a satisfactory one, but it is as I saw life at the time."

Rebekkah wipes a tear from her eye, still greatly affected by her past experiences, "The Doctor had left the country each time, taking on a new name and identity. I couldn't track him down until I realized I was tracing the wrong thing. I needed to trace the drug. Certain Doctors get used to using certain drugs, and they often stick with the same drug companies. The Doctors get familiar with these drugs, and they prescribe them in like doses and in like combinations with other drugs. It's like a blueprint of the Doctor's preferred choices, the Doctor's prescribed comfort. That in itself would usually be of little help, though the drug I was searching for was so rarely used, I felt I may be able to trace it. Algorithms and such can be a very helpful thing, yet like most things ...can be abused, and it could be said that I was breaching their privacy and confidentiality. Yet, I ran a computer check, and I got a couple dozen Doctors who came close in my search. The thing that got my attention was that three of the Doctors were at the same facility. But what shocked me the most was the name of the facility—-Huron Valley Center prison. And they were practicing under the direction of Frank Bodin. But most concerning was the fact that my best friend's son was working there. Frank covered his tracks fairly well. I was convinced that he was the same Doctor I'd been looking for, but my suspicions were too loose. The facts were not enough to convince anyone, but I was convinced. I was certain that he was involved in other illegal activities also. Those who do great wrongs, are usually guilty on many levels. But I needed help to prove that. And that's where Lisa Stone came in."

Rebekkah stands briefly, then sits back down, "I had already done my homework. Several of the prisoners were not mentally ill, they were not even prisoners. They were a select group of talented young men ...and they were able to work covertly without fear of being exposed. What better place to run his scam than inside a high security prison! Some of them approached the genius of Stan Olitz, when it came to computers. And Frank was using them, as a means to further his needs through computer fraud ...with a disturbingly long list of cybercrimes. That's the charge Lisa Stone helped me get him on—-and he was convicted on it, and sent to prison. This time he would not leave from inside the prison walls ...he would be confined within them. But I felt Lisa's life had become increasingly more dangerous for her upon Frank's conviction. She was to benefit from the Witness Protection Program, but she disappeared before they could arrange for her disappearance. I helped her disappear. We could not be certain whether Frank Bodin had worked independently, for his own personal gain. But we were certain he had gained sufficient wealth and influence, he could easily pay someone to get revenge on Lisa for testifying."

You can tell making this tape was hard on Rebekkah. Her right eye begins to twitch. One would perhaps wonder whether she is going to have a stroke during this taping. You can tell it was bothering her.

She hits her eye a couple times with a brush of her hand, but she continues to focus on what she is driven to say, "As the years passed, my life did not fill itself with pleasantries. Tragedy after tragedy seemed to happen. The one person who had caused me so much pain, was locked up ...but I was not satisfied. I tried to work on my own anger problem. Why were things continuing to happen? Maybe God was not pleased with me. That would be easy to imagine, since—-I was not pleased with myself. This sort of destructive thinking can follow you to the grave, and it nearly did. I sincerely felt my time had finally come ...as I went to the hospital. But my time here on earth was obviously not complete. That's when it finally happened!"

Rebekkah coughs, then takes a drink of water, "George...", again, coughing .... "George Olitz came to the hospital to be with me. He had a fainting episode and a bad fall. He was delirious and mumbling. His mumbling made no sense to me at the time. It appeared to me to be just a lot of senseless confusion. But for some reason, I felt much unrest about it. I could not get it out of my mind. Then came the accidental discovery. There was a DNA match-up between George Olitz and Crazy Larry. But that was only the tip of the iceberg. More weird things had happened. Frank Bodin was shipped to the prison hospital. They could not help him. He died quickly. A very large dose of the very same drug that he had prescribed for years, was in his system. That same drug that could be used to retard recovery, when used in a large dose, could speed up the progression to death. That's when I made the connection between Frank and what George was saying. Finally, it was all beginning to come together."

Rebekkah coughs, "Excuse me, I am quite tired, but I want to finish this taping."

She coughs again, then gasps. It appears doubtful that she can go on much longer, yet she composes herself enough to continue, "Everything began to happen at once. I have my own complicated method to relay information to Lisa Stone. Lisa attempted to sort it out for me. Yet, my biggest finding was accidental ...or perhaps not. Maybe God wanted me to know. I was just checking in on a friend—-my friend, George—-when I saw he was about to pass out. He was in a stupor in front of his personal computer, possibly having a stroke. What I found was not just a stroke of good luck. I believe I was meant to find it. I printed it off his computer. There were notes of a very disturbing nature: '*Coercive Psychological Methods, a Means to an End, Maximizing Personal Gain at the Expense of a Failing Government System*.' That seemed like nothing more than a bunch of mumbo jumbo, but when I began reading the article, I couldn't believe what it actually said."

Rebekkah leans forward in her seat, not looking well, but determined to finish this tape that will be shared sometime after her death, the time of which she will be unaware, but which happens to be now, "Now the doctors say George is debilitating quickly. I intended to have my own private test done ...and when I did, it was discovered that George had that same drug in his system to expedite his death. Yet, it was already too late to prevent it. Now, all this information has not benefited me one bit. It has saddened me. Too often I have been angry. But what did it benefit me? Well, *that* I am sure to tell you ...I believe this revelation was not meant for my benefit. It was meant for me to pass on to you. Knowing that it may serve some purpose that I don't know about, comforts me at this time. Perhaps many of you are soon going to have to make an important choice. And I believe there are certain things you should know before making that choice."

*** * * * * ***

Stan Olitz and the President are still at that special celebratory dinner, when an Aide to the President rushes in to tell of the news being viewed across everyone's computer screens. Stan and the President excuse themselves. They find a private room and click on the computer, viewing the large screen. Sweat now gathers quickly across Stan's brow.

Rebekkah sets her conclusion, "Many of you may question why I am using my last gasping breaths to tell you all of this ...when upon finding these things out I could have just removed George and Stan Olitz from their corporate positions. Well, yes, forbid the thought that perhaps the horror is now unfolding ...but, I would not have been able to stop it. The only way it can be stopped is if the one who is creating this havoc chooses to stop it. And if I had dismantled all the corporate workings, then I would have destroyed all means for the possibility that it could be stopped. And that is why I've left the extensive corporate structure intact ...and for these last few moments of mine, I have spent way too much time explaining all the wrongs that have taken place. What I really want is to extend a heartfelt appeal. Relationships are not supposed to exist for the purpose of creating a means to an end. And I would suggest an end to the meanness, but that's up to you, Stan."

Rebekkah concludes her conclusion, "George saw things as a means to an end. Yet, I'm now pleading with you to end this, Stan. George was interested in you because he saw your potential for genius, just like he saw the potential for my great wealth. I hesitate to thank him for helping you realize your potential. What George became, he was grooming you to become. And yes, George was human just like we are ...and somewhere within him, I believe he did care for me and for you, Stan. But, somehow it seems George grew up not really believing anyone could sustain loving him for any length of time ...so he tried to control others to guard against the possibility of anyone again abandoning him. But, I don't think he quite understood the difference between deserting him and merely rejecting his ideas. I hope you see that we cannot support anyone who chooses to go down this path. Now it is your turn, Stan, to choose whether you want to guide others toward potential good, or lead them away from it. Your choice ...to be a mentor, or a tormentor. My plea is for you to not seek your own kingdom, but to inherit the Kingdom of God."

Rebekkah grimaces. She falls to the side in her chair, then out of view.

The tape temporarily becomes 'flashes and specks', then Lisa Stone returns back to the screen. For added effect, she puts her disguise back on, beard and glasses. Her accent returns as she speaks, "And the segment that you just saw was sent a while ago to Stan. If he had accepted the appeal, none of you would have seen this tape. I was only supposed to release this if Stan made the wrong choice. Now, the choice is not only Stan's. The entire world must make their own choice. Right now there is a call to join together as a nation in the name of patriotism. We claim that the highest honor we can bestow upon anyone is in reference to national loyalty ...those who fight for their own country, preserving the love of country through their devotion and purpose, and through their sacrifice for their country. The opposite of a patriot is: One who breaks faith with, fails to meet the hopes of, and leads others astray through deceitful words and practices. That betrayal of one's own country, cause, or friends—-is usually considered unforgivable, and that person is labeled a traitor. Who is it that breaks the trust, love, and loyalty for one's country? It depends who you are listening to ...and what your vision for your nation is. Saying this will likely have little effect upon most of you ...other than dismissing my words, or relegating my statements to the mere status of a crazy person. And I admit, it does seem crazy—-but, that's just it—-there is so much at play to potentially deceive you. Be honest, would you have trusted me more if I hadn't initially addressed you with my disguise on? I doubt that it would have made a difference ...as most of you have already decided who you trust."

Lisa removes her disguise again, "People like me are quickly labeled as conspiracy theorists, QAnon advocates, or 'deniers' ...and are discredited, and laughed at. But look at the world right now ...I don't see anyone laughing. And as you recall, I haven't reported any conspiracies ...I'm only now speaking up. And if you need some more evidence, I'm providing a 'link' to poor misguided George's article, referencing his plan. I know some of you are smart enough to copy it ...as you know it will soon be taken down. Yes, I know people like me are often discredited. Grouping me with people whom I myself disagree with ...how conveniently that labels me as 'just one of them'. And what an awesome job the major news networks do ...a large portion of it is about how stupid someone else is. And if the media is saturated with all the stupid stuff someone else is doing or saying, then their own stupid stuff goes relatively undetected. Their own wild ideas are presented as sound reasoning at this point, and their claims become more palatable. Falsehoods are welcomed, and are actually promoted as a plus for a negative group who get most of the media attention, denying that they're in fact ...'deniers' of so much of what is true. Already accustomed to and comfortable with ridiculing others, they stand ready to discredit those who don't agree with them. And because it works so cleverly this way ...that's why we didn't report before what I am now exposing. Again, be honest ...would you have believed me? Maybe now you will take notice! Tragedy often stokes the fires of fear ...and that lingering fear readily embraces compliance. And why do you think churches were called upon to help? It is because churches want to help, they feel called to help ...and once the churches get on board, then people will more likely feel inclined to follow. But let me be clear ...there is a hidden agenda. There are many big businesses and companies within our nation who have done much to lead us astray and deceive us ...not just because of greed, but for motives too diabolical to understand or describe.

But that's why I've listed the 'link', so you can download it and read it yourself. I don't know what drives such ruthless lust for power—-but once it begins, it doesn't need any help—-it thrives, and drives itself. It only takes a few willing people for evil to thrive, but we must stand together for the truth to prevail."

Lisa gets to the heart of the matter, "And yes, the 'political' often gets our attention ...how can it not, especially during a crisis as we are now facing. Yes, it is important that we can come out of this together ...yet, however this plays out, there is something else important we want to share. Yes, there is another crisis that we often don't consider ...one that has been developing for years. We claim we are evolving intellectually, yet we are redefining our spiritual life. How wise is that? Can we not see the growing unbelief or disbelief? Whatever we call it, it is still not believing. And those who say they believe, and say they follow the 'Essence' ...that just adds to the confusion. It is part of the deception. The Bible is the source of truth. But what the truth has become, we have allowed it to become. Why is God now often either listed as a small *'g'*, or *generic*—-and Jesus is often known as someone who told many parables—-but today His stories are not even considered popular ones? Yes, it is confusing ...you may ask, would I be so bold as to say it's clearly evil. I know, most of you don't like the word 'evil', but in short, evil is that which opposes God ...opposing that which is good and right. And yes, many wrong things have been done while claiming God is behind it ... and many of those things I do not stand with, nor do I believe God is with them on those things. So, please don't point to people ...as if the fringe people represent what Jesus would have us do. Those many people didn't represent Jesus some two thousand years ago ...and many don't today. Look to the Bible, to read about Jesus—-and read about what the disciples of Jesus said. Reflect on things of eternal value. Too often we develop our own kingdom building. Do you believe the one who has the vision of that kingdom should control the kingdom? You've just voted to give that control to Stan. You have put your faith in Stan's promised plan of salvation for our economy and the security of our nation—-yet, do you even acknowledge any substance of eternal security through God's plan of salvation?"

Lisa sounds quite passionate about what she is saying, in spite of her now even more pronounced accent, "I cannot stress this enough. You would readily call me ignorant, foolish, and stubborn. Like Balaam, you'd blame the donkey, when you are actually the stubborn one. But sadly enough, most of you don't even know who Balaam is. For years, you have turned away from the Bible and stubbornly ignored the truth. The majority of you no longer believe in the truth. You believe in 'the Essence', which in essence, is to believe in whatever you want to believe in. You are like those described in the Book of Judges ...believing that whatever you see fit in your own eyes is sufficient."

Lisa turns to another page in the Bible, but seems to know her reference without having to read it, "And your condition is also quite accurately described in the first Chapter of the Book of Romans ...as you've been roamin' around, looking for whatever it is that satisfies your whims: *'Because when they knew God, they glorified Him not as God, neither were thankful; but became vain in their imaginations ...changed the glory of the incorruptible God onto an image made like to corruptible man. So God gave you up to uncleanness through the lusts of your own hearts.'* We chose to deceive ourselves ...now we can easily be deceived by others."

Lisa leaves her Bible open, but looks up, "Do we believe in the technological truth claims? Do you know that each one of you is being profiled? Do you know how an algorithm works? And what about censorship? I never experienced what my parents did, yet in their day there was a quite powerful organization called the PTA—-Parent-Teacher Association. They had much influence with what was on television, and they promoted healthy standards for our youth. But now, often what is good is being censored ...much in the name of personal rights. And it is at our local, state, and federal levels of government. Spreading disinformation is on the list of federal crimes ...and that is politically charged to mean whatever they want it to mean."

A hand extends in front of the camera, placing a vase of flowers beside Lisa, "Oh, thank you ...they are really pretty. Oh, but they are artificial ...and everyone knows what that means. They are not real, they are fake ...so, I don't have to worry about if they'll live. That being said, what does 'artificial' intelligence (AI) mean?? Is the concept fake ...because whatever is deemed as 'intelligence' is created by someone? And isn't it all tied in with that 'chip' many of you are getting? There seems to be no avenue for discretion given to us through the Holy Spirit, providing for us the wisdom of 'correct use of knowledge' ...we are only to proclaim and submit to a higher intelligence, created through man's programming."

Lisa talks in her best robotic voice, "You pro-claim to be our lead-er, but you are ig-nor-ant and mis-in-formed. We gath-er in-for-mation to a-chieve perr-fec-tion. In-for-ma-tion-al Tow-er of Bab-bel ...bab-ble. bab-ble, psycho-bab-ble, sound-ing brass-s-s, tink-ling-ling cym-bol ...dis-guised by our sym-bol of free-dom. Free-dumb is sym-bol of sim-ple-mind-ed who thin-k-k free to spea-k-k can-not be ter-min-nated by me."

The camera focuses in ...on the Bible resting on the table in front of Lisa, "We may say we have the same source of truth, but we still present great differences. Now, I have one more thing to say. Jesus instructed His disciples to spread the 'good news' of salvation, led in truth by the Holy Spirit. And if the disciples encountered those who would not receive the words of salvation given to them through Jesus, there are always many others who will gladly embrace the truth. Yet, what can be said of today? There are those who say the Bible is outdated. They say there are new truths and revelations. And if *they* are not received, they act as if the ones in error are the ones who don't embrace what *they* say. And as time goes on, we are asked to believe many other things. Is this where we falter and become way too political again? I caution you—-be careful with your discernment. Do you accept any self-ordained authority over Christ's? And I'd have to ask one more thing: Are they judging beyond Jesus, as if there are qualifications for salvation beyond His love, beyond His sacrifice for us, and beyond His Word? The disciples of Jesus did not blindly follow, and His Word in the Bible should be our guide in Truth. To not hold the Bible as our authority for Truth, is not a testimony to God, but merely to ourselves only."

The camera moves about the room, showing all the residents from the walled community; an additional community—-an entire orphan population, supervised by Angelo; and most of Missionary Island's past residents.

This time Rebekkah's son, Stephen, speaks, "We realize how truly confusing this may all be. Our main intent is not to focus on the lies and deception, but to bring light to the truth. Therefore, it may be beneficial to back up a bit—-to take a look at how it all began, to see when things were right, and to realize when the right could no longer be discerned from the wrong—-and why that is. We have purposed together to show you why that is—-to bring you the truth, and allow you to see how we have moved away from that truth to this confusion we now all live in. Our story, *'The Evolution of Confusion,'* is only purposed to bring attention to His story, the only significant history that benefits us, beyond the past, to the present, and eternally into the future."

Stephen extends a hand to his wife. Maggie concludes, "Many of you refused to make the full commitment years ago. You didn't just reap the benefits of technology—-you let it change your life. You let the distractions occupy too much of your lives. You let science not be science, but a study of selective preferences. And you think God has to submit to it all—-or you think He has to merely function within our own wisdom. We became wise in our own conceits. Now the choice is a more difficult choice for many of you. There may be unpleasant consequences for many of you for making the right choice. For some of you, that may make it a bit difficult. But some of you have a tendency to be difficult. For me, the choice is easy. We must all choose. Some of you may decide not to choose. That is not an option. By not choosing, you are still choosing."

Shannon and Leah sit down together.

Shannon appeals, "Oh, Stan ...we had attended those classes together, then were baptized together on that special day soon afterwards. We both professed that we believe Jesus sacrificed His own life ...yes, He died so we can be saved. Saved from what? Well ...who is happy with how the earth is now? We need to be saved from this madness ...but, we don't know if we are going to be spared from what is happening now. What we can look forward to ...is that we can be spared from this happening over and over again, for eternity. Heaven will not have this kind of madness. And if we want to be with God for eternity, then why would we not want to be with Him now?"

Leah adds, "Stan ...none of us are judging you. I'm not even challenging you ...what I'm doing is appealing to you, to accept God's salvation. Fernye saved you from the fire that took the rest of your family. And while you were saving Ray and Claudia's baby, the riverbank collapsed—-and you got swept up in the current. Then George saved you. Most everyone loved you, Stan—-and you seemed to love us. Yet, what Fernye and George did, and what you did for Ray and Claudia's child—-as loving as it is to save each other in this life, it does not equate with us being 'saved' for eternity."

Josiah stands behind Leah and Shannon, resting a hand on each of their shoulders, "Let me give a little personal history, not to just you, Stan, but to everyone. A few generations ago, Dad's mom feared her own dad—-Roy Razohn. She didn't fear him because of a misunderstanding ...she had much reason to fear him. People used to fear God too, but for different reasons. They didn't really know Him. They saw what God could do, and they feared Him. Dad's mom also saw what her dad could do. Roy Razohn demanded respect. Thinking that there has to be fear for there to be 'respect' ...well, that is not true. It is better to 'respect' out of love."

Samuel stands alongside, joining his brother, "I never feared Dad while growing up ...as he wasn't here. I witnessed the love from my older brother and sisters ...and the videos helped too. What I feared was a doubt that I should never have allowed to creep into my head ...a fear that perhaps Dad would not love me. I collected all the clippings from articles about Dad's disappearance ...and most of them were not favorable. I had to look at what I was told by those who 'knew' him, and try to not get taken down the path of those who care much less about 'truth' and more about creating mere sensationalism. And even though I embraced the moments that Shannon had video-taped ...there had to be more. I needed more. When God's people fled slavery in Egypt, they wandered in the desert. They had memories—-and they didn't have a video to hold their memories, but they built an Ark of the Covenant—-and put memories in it; including the manna God had provided them, the rod of Aaron that had budded, and two tablets bearing the Ten Commandments. After that, they were given more to guide them ...as God dictated to Moses what to tell the people. Though, just like us, the people often didn't follow what they said they believed. I'll let Joe tell you more ...he's good with reasoning that part."

Josiah pats him on the back, "You do fine, Sam ...like you said, God told Moses what to write. So many people have said that Moses didn't understand what we understand today, so he just wrote it the way he observed it. But, Moses wasn't around when everything happened in the beginning, and I'm referring to the first couple Chapters of Genesis. He wrote of what God had him write. And other people say that Moses wasn't around at all, or that it was an overinflated image that Moses had of himself while recalling his journeys. Or they say that the story of Noah was copied from earlier stories like the 'Epic of Gilgamesh' (which in actuality was written around the time of the Tower of Babel). Does it occur to them that all the other writings were about an actual event, and perhaps God had Moses clearly write the details to clear up the confusion about that actual event? Jesus also spoke of Moses—-in the Gospel of John, Chapter 5, verses 46 & 47—-*'For had you believed Moses, you would have believed Me; for he wrote of Me. But if you believe not his writings, how shall you believe My words.'* And to that ...they say those verses are corrupted, as they are not the Synoptic Gospels, and it is doubtful Moses even existed. Yet, if you look into the Synoptic Gospels—-Chapter 17 of Matthew; and Chapter 9 of both Mark and Luke—-all three do speak of the transfiguration, where both Moses and Elijah appear with Jesus. So, if the Gospel of John is thought to be corrupted, and Matthew, Mark, and Luke cannot accurately describe or quote Jesus—-then what do we trust as our source of believing at all?"

Stephen stands between Josiah and Samuel, putting a loving arm around them and giving them a pat of approval on the back. "There is a part of the Bible that I have pondered much about. In the Gospels, if I recall, I think it is also in Matthew. Thank you, Josiah—-he was just holding up seven fingers, so it would be in the 7th Chapter of Matthew where Jesus tells of people calling Him, Lord,—-and doing many wonders in His Name, yet He says He never knew them. The first part of the Chapter says to 'judge not', and I am not judging anyone ...it is just a concern of mine. And what does it mean 'to know'?"

Samuel gives Dad a side hug, "Sorry to interrupt, Dad ...but, I think this is where I come in. A person can know certain things by hearing of them. I knew about you, but you didn't know I existed. In my case, 'knowing' was something that was shared with me ...as we couldn't interact. On the other hand, God knows everything about all of us, so to those He would say 'He never knew them', it is not like areas of the earth where they haven't heard ...I believe God looks at their understanding a bit different. And from what we hear from missionaries, like Shannon here, when those people hear of salvation through Jesus, they more readily receive and embrace that truth than many of us who have heard many times over and over. Yet, the verse you mentioned doesn't appear to be addressing the people who have not heard, and who don't yet 'know'. As you quoted, the Bible says they were calling Him, Lord ...and doing many wonders in His Name. That sounds like it's more about them, than about our Lord. Were they glorifying themselves? Isn't the 'knowing' supposed to be a 'developing' relationship ...a two-way relationship, with us accepting Him for who He is, not attempting to tailor Him to our liking? The way I see it, what I read in the Bible is much to my liking ...so, why would I even want to look at it in a different way?"

Cindy slips in, snuggling between Shannon and Leah—-and shares some very special news, "Speaking of *'two'*, of *'knowing'*, and of *'liking'*—-I decided not to wait to tell Dad this time. I just found out, and shared it last evening with him—-that we are going to have another child. I'm obviously not too old, and we will hopefully do the full 'training up the child' together this time. When our baby comes, either he or she, will be told about God ...and for certain *'know'* how we believe."

Upon hearing the news of another sibling for the first time, Leah and Shannon snuggle close to Mom, and Josiah and Samuel put an arm around Dad.

Stephen increases the embrace with an arm around his sons, then lovingly leans forward ...moving them into a huge hug of six ...actually, seven.

Cindy turns around and smiles at Stephen, "I'm so grateful that our entire family has accepted the salvation message of Jesus. I am also happy to truly *know* you love me ...and that you *know* how very much I love you."

The camera pans away as Stephen and Cindy kiss ...

The camera focuses on one person standing alone. But, he has a big grin on his face. It is Larry.

Larry eagerly shares, "My entire life so many people said that I was crazy, but I'm so thankful for this family ...and all the things they have shared with me. I think one would be crazy not to believe. Well, maybe not crazy ...but certainly it would be so sad. The Bible tells us what we need to believe. Many of my friends here have mentioned that we should all *'know'* God. With the Bible, we have a rich history of His love, which is also affirmed by Jesus being born as man—-to soon correct the ways that had gone wrong, and to set us on the path to truth—-the path of salvation. The truth of Jesus has been preserved for us—-and we have the awesome opportunity to believe. There have been so many choices in my life that were made for me—-and most of that was not a good thing. But I'm thrilled to be able to make this choice myself. Each of you can make the same choice—-we all have the same opportunity. We can all *know* —-*'we should know'*. And we should tell others so they too can know ...*know* Him."

Epilogue:

Fear may make a stand ...to keep you from the truth.
　　But once you've embraced *truth*, continue to do so.
　　If 'truth' rules the day, fear will not drive you away.

True love is the love of truth. That love will keep you.

The secret is to find *'truth'*.
　　It is not difficult to find.
　　It is merely found by the sincere seeking of it.
　　It was not meant to be a secret.

Its purpose is to be sought.
　　We share it so others may seek it.
　　Those who don't share it ...are robbing it of its purpose.

Yet, we may differ with what we believe *'truth'* is.
　　The heart and the mind may lead us astray.
　　But there is sincerity and truth in the Words of Jesus.
　　And this 'we should know' ...

* * * * * * * * * * * * * * * *

Fear is the beginning of wisdom.
Love allows you to finish the race.

Let me explain.

* * * * * * * *

Fear is the beginning of wisdom.

I fear not listening to Dad. My Dad does not believe in spanking. He says his own dad believed in a whipping, not a spanking. He said Grandpa used a milker strap, or milking strap—-something like that. It was a thick leather strap with metal eyelets, to fasten the belt around the cow, which the milker was attached to. Dad has a thick leather belt that he wears. He used it on me once. I can't imagine what Grandpa's strap felt like. It must have really hurt. Dad says he behaved when he was young because he feared the strap.

I thought about that.

At the time, I thought I would even prefer the strap—-to what Dad began to use. He used his mind. He made me sit a time out, which I thought was a terrible thing for a boy like me who has so much energy. And worse yet, while I was sitting there, Dad would make me think about what I did. I thought to myself, "I think I'd prefer the strap. Sure it would hurt, but it would be much quicker."

That was not the end of it either. The worst part was that I would have to tell all about what happened.

Yes, as if thinking about it was not painful enough, I'd have to go through the pain all over again by talking about it afterwards. So, I was really afraid that I might get a time out.

Once I told Dad that, but he said I didn't fear it enough—-since I still didn't avoid it. Dad had a point there. I had a real problem with my focus. If I feared it so much, then why didn't I think about that in advance—-and avoid the trouble?

When I turned 13 years old, or years young, as Dad would say, I asked him when I would get years old. Dad said, "When you act like it."

Well, this particular day I felt old. Dad took me with him to the woods when he went for firewood. He brought his chainsaw and some earplugs, so the loud chainsaw wouldn't damage his hearing, he said. Dad said I wasn't old enough to operate a chainsaw, but I felt kind of old, just by the sole fact that Dad took me along.

Somewhere along the way though, I must've begun feeling young again.

Dad warned me of bears in the woods, and not to wander off. But, my young self got bored with watching Dad. I could think of more pleasant things than standing there while sawdust and woodchips kept flying in my face.

So, I wandered off.

I must *not* have been thinking of the time out, or worse yet, the talk afterwards ...or even worse, the chance meeting with a bear, which would perhaps remind me of my disobedience—-in perhaps a much more severe fashion.

Nevertheless, I sadly have to admit that I wandered off. And sure enough, there was a bear. I saw the bear before he saw me. I also quickly saw the wisdom in fearing to disobey Dad. But since I hadn't respected that fear, I now faced a greater fear—-the quick wisdom and fear that comes naturally, in facing the bear.

I was already running as fast as I could, but I knew I could never outrun the bear. I thought I had a good head start, but when the bear began to give chase, I realized I had no chance in running from the bear.

A change came over me then. I found myself, not running *from* the bear, but rather running *to* my Dad.

I was afraid because I disobeyed Dad, but this was the very first time I eagerly awaited my time out—-and *the 'talk'*.

I now saw Dad differently than I had before. I really believe Dad doesn't enjoy giving me time outs. He stresses obedience, and is so rigid with his standards because he loves me. And that's why I ran to him—-not fearing the time out.

Of course, this time Dad not only had me talk about the incident, but he also made me write about it. I had to re-write it five times! Anyway, you've just read the story. I know it's not a long story. By now, you probably know what it's like to read a long story. But I thought I could make my point with a 5-page story, listing only the *'bear'* facts.

Today, I have a bear rug to step onto as I crawl out of bed on cold winter mornings. And I don't dread time outs, or the talk afterwards. Actually, I find myself talking to Dad more freely. I ask for a time out to talk with him when I'm troubled about having done something wrong. And I do something else I've never done. I cry when I feel I've really disappointed Dad.

It may have taken fear to bring me to this point, but it wasn't fearing him ...it was the fear of realizing what could have happened if I hadn't turned to him in my time of need. I now know how much he loves me, and the thing that matters to me the most, is that I please him.

And I listen closer to some of the even more important things that Dad has tried in the past to talk with me about. Before I had heard some, but didn't listen much. But now, I think I am even beginning to understand.

****

The fear of God is the beginning of wisdom.

But the end is the love of God ...which never ends.

* * * * * * * *

When I built anything around the house, it was always crude, yet functional. It certainly was not attractive. I feel the same way about my writing. I hope it provides some function.

This is an obvious dedication to my wife and children. They have put up with me and endured a tired Dad who stayed up late at night, so as not to interfere with 'time with Dad' during the day. I guess the greatest sacrifice came from my wife whom I missed so dearly during those long nights. That was supposed to be our time—-our quiet time, together.

But instead of getting complaints, I received another gift. That gift we have already decided to name 'David'. As I am finishing up this book, he is only two weeks away from being born. (Of course, there have been a couple decades between 'finished' writing and actual publishing ...so, though he is our youngest, he is already an adult now.)

I was not able to write him into the story, yet he is a wonderful chapter in our lives. And there is one book that we count on him being mentioned in—-The Book of Life.

* * * * * * * *

As children, most all of us drew pictures and gave them to our parents. Perhaps they hugged us, kissed us, or perhaps both. Rest assured, they thanked us with various forms of affirmation and affection.

Sadly, not all children get that loving treatment. But I did. And I'm thankful for it. But what would really make me feel important, was when my parents placed my drawing where everyone could see it—-the most important place in the house—-on the refrigerator. It had to be the most important place—-it held all those treasures. And the most treasured of all treasures were those mouthwatering 'Ting-a-lings'. You guessed it, they were made with one of my favorite ingredients—-chocolate. I'll have to give Mom a call and get you the recipe.

Anyway, my sole picture remained there for weeks on the refrigerator. I felt so special. I didn't realize my parents' apparent concern though. My parents weren't disturbed by my drawing. Let me just say, they had loving concern. But they didn't verbalize their concerns. The old standby was, "He will grow out of it, eventually."

And grow, I did. Now things have come full-circle. My children are drawing me pictures for the refrigerator. As for me, well, I've advanced from drawing pictures to writing books. And now my parents are able to verbalize what they perhaps were unable to when I was young. After reading this over 900-page series, they wrote me, "You have an amazing imagination."

Now there's that word of curious popularity. Pastor also used the word ..."Simply amazing!" Honestly, I don't know what was being emphasized ...'simple' or 'amazing'.

Anyway, I am a grown-up now. At least that is my perception of it. And I'd like an honest critique. Has my writing graduated beyond the prestige of my refrigerator drawings?

If not, then at least try the recipe I made reference to in the story, 'The Princess and the Poppy'. And yes, I do think those mouthwatering Ting-a-lings are good, but they are not the most treasured of treasures. *"For where your treasure is, there will your heart be also." (Matthew 6:21)*

Ting-a-lings

Ingredients: One box of flake cereal (my preference, *Wheaties*) & one 12 ounce bag of chocolate chips (my preference being the semi-sweet dark chocolate, or special dark chocolate)

Preparation: Put wax paper on a couple cookie trays and make sure a space is cleared in the refrigerator to place the trays in, once the cookies are made. [You'll need a fairly large casserole dish, a large zip-lock bag, a measuring cup, a regular teaspoon, and preferably a rolling pin.]

Begin: Measure out 6 cups of uncrushed flakes into the zip-lock bag. Use the rolling pin (or the palm of your hand) to crush the flakes. Crush them into fine pieces, but not into dust. Empty the 12 ounces of chocolate chips into the casserole dish, and heat them on medium power for a minute in the microwave. Take them out and stir (if you can), then place back into the microwave for a minute and a half. Take the dish out and stir immediately. Then add the entire bag of crushed flakes. Stir thoroughly, as if you were mixing cement and gravel (note especially for men). Take a regular teaspoon or a measuring spoon, and scoop up that portion to place on the cookie sheet. (By the way, hopefully you've already washed your hands, and don't lick your fingers until after you are done.) Then place the filled cookie sheets in the refrigerator.

The laborer's appetizer: You've done the work, now you can lick the bowl.

The experience: When the cookies harden, you can stack them in another container, as *not* to take up as much space. And of course, you eat some ...that will take up even less space in the refrigerator. But restraint is the key! Always leave enough to be served to others.

The real experience: Psalm 119:103-105, "How sweet are thy words unto my taste! Yea, sweeter than honey to my mouth. Through thy precepts I get understanding: therefore I hate every false way. Thy word is a lamp unto my feet, and a light unto my path."

***serve others with His truth,
   and they will be truly served ***

* * * * * * I also write under the pen name of Shepherd Heath. Several years ago our German Shepherd, named Heath, got out by way of our gate and he decided to explore, but got hit by a car. During Homeschooling our children, we were practicing writing stories and at that time I began using the pen name, in memory of our dog.* * * * * *

Now, I feel I must add the second part of the story 'The Princess and the Poppy':

"Sweetie, thank you so much for this priceless moment. Our kingdom has experienced an unprecedented three hundred years of peace now, but no greater peace does any king have than the inner peace a dad feels when experiencing the warmth of appreciation from a loving child."

King Lee no sooner speaks those words ...when his Royal Subject bursts onto the scene nearly out of breath, "Your Excellency, I've just received word from a messenger of King Aling."

King Lee is still feeling the warmth of the moment with his daughter, Shannon ..."Ah, yes, King Aling ...a very wise and dear friend. Often he has comforted me with his wise counsel ...what message does he send?"

The messenger does not seem as if he is one about to share any comforting news, but is as one carrying a heavy burden. He catches his breath, "King Aling's daughter, Ting ...has up and vanished."

King Lee knows what this means, "I must go to him at once ...alone."

The Royal Subject, "Is that wise, Your Excellency?"

King Lee, "This urgency does not lend time for wisdom ...he is a loyal friend, and I must go at once. You are my loyal friend also, and I trust you will safely escort Shannon back to my castle immediately!"

King Lee talks softly to his horse, hoping his horse can somehow understand that his usual kindness in providing adequate rest for a journey ...is now being sacrificed. As he approaches Aling's kingdom, King Lee sees smoke billowing in the far distance. He must hurry!!

Just outside the castle walls, the devastation reveals itself. He stands strong and ready for battle, yet faint. There are fifteen who had stood bravely with undying courage for however long the battle, but now all that remains is a lifeless testimony to that which each had given their life to defend.

King Lee rushes beyond this point, swiftly moving within the castle walls ...looking for any sign of life, and his friend, Aling.

Suddenly, he sees movement ...and he hesitates, attempting to conceal his presence. He isn't sure if the person had also seen him ...yet, it appears the person has no weapon.

The young man kneels beside a motionless body ...with a crown!!

King Lee calls out, "King Aling!"

The young man looks up, sobbing, "They've killed my father!"

King Lee kneels down also, checking for signs of life ...but, there are none. He then stands there for quite some time, as the young man continues to kneel, holding his dear friend, King Aling, in his arms while sobbing over and over again, "Father ...Father ...."

Suddenly, there is cause for disturbance. Entering the room, covered in dirt and blood, is King Lee's Royal Subject. "They've taken Shannon!! I'm so sorry ...I am disgraced that I am still alive. I am not deserving to stand before you; with every breath of life, I should have prevented it. I have failed you, Your Excellency!"

King Lee is overcome with emotion, but takes a deep breath, "I know you did your best ...don't blame yourself."

King Lee realizes that it may be too dangerous to act impulsively with his present emotion. That could merely put Shannon's life more in danger. He takes the long painful journey back to his castle ...and the whole way back, he tries to devise a plan in his head.

As he returns to his castle, King Lee introduces the young man to his own son. "You will stand beside my son ...and be as my very own son."

King Lee's son hugs the young man, "It has been way too long since our families have been together ...and you have certainly grown since we last got together. I guess we both have ...but, oh, how insensitive of me to speak of trifling details at such a time as this. I am deeply sorry for what happened to your father."

The young man looks down, "Yes, it was horrible!! I wish I had been with the others in battle ...to prevent it."

King Lee's son rests his hand on the young man's shoulder, "I have been all these years an only son, but now you are my brother. We will stand together and fight. We've had peace so long, we have no army ...but, our people will come together now to fight ...and you will stand beside me in battle."

King Lee is proud of his son's bravery, but he chooses his words carefully, "We are not to be too hasty with our decisions. All the courage in the entire world will not account for much if not tempered with sought out wisdom. I am certain that we could take on the enemy and be assured of victory, but what are we to celebrate victory in? If we are to take up a noble cause, are we to lose sight of our goal? Most certainly, I believe that in achieving victory over the enemy, it would be at the cost of Shannon's life. They would not accept defeat without first taking her life."

That thought is cause for a long period of silence. Then the young man speaks up, "Yesterday, I lost my father. Today, you've accepted me as your son. I want to have a chance to prove I am worthy and deserving. I will go alone. I will have a better chance of rescuing Shannon if too much attention is not drawn. I know how to dress like a common person ...and I don't think they will suspect me."

King Lee nods, "I agree that we have the best chance with your plan. You may go alone, my son."

"No, I should go! They have my sister ...I will go alone!"

King Lee touches his son on the shoulder, "No, son, you look too much like me. You will have no chance in pulling it off. Today, you have gained a brother and I have gained a son. We have both gained a friend. We will accept his brave offer."

****

Several weeks go by ...and hope becomes a distant subject, too painful to even discuss.

King Lee appears to be the only one to still hold hope in his heart, yet it is difficult to say, since they don't discuss it. Yet, at the dawn of each new day, there is no new news ...and King Lee knows his own hope is vanishing.

As the day is about spent, King Lee once again looks out his window from the highest point of his castle, as he does every evening just as the sun begins to set.

His eyes are tired. He has not slept much since Shannon has been gone.

It is a brilliant sunset this evening. The bright pinks and reds splash against a fading blue sky. And shadows reach out across the landscape, grasping for and gathering in the last remnants of light.

The trickery of the shadows have their last moment of frolic, before they play themselves out. And tired eyes lose touch with reality amongst a host of heartfelt wishful thinking.

One last moment of trickery ...before all is overcome with darkness.

Three deer find their way to feed at the edge of the meadow. The deer move slowly into the meadow ...taking on the form of mere shadows ...of humans? Can it be??

King Lee leaps down the castle stairs, skipping most of the steps ...and almost falling.

He stumbles out the castle doors, sprinting out into the meadow.

The young man has returned ...with Shannon!! And the third person ...is Ting!!

The sun has left them, but the castle chases out all the shadows as it lights up in celebration of their return.

****

The celebration carries on into the next day.

As the bird's sing to the dawning of another day, King Lee announces, "I believe our three celebrities must be in need of much sleep ...but, I do not believe they will get much rest unless we all agree to get some rest."

As everyone then beds down for not the night, but for the light ...the castle becomes very quiet. No one hears King Lee still moving about. He feels he must do one more thing before he can sleep.

He stands in the doorway for several minutes ...before the young man notices him. King Lee speaks softly, "I want to thank you again, my son. I know what a difficult thing it must have been for you."

The young man has tears in his eyes, "I have a confession to make. I was not going to return. I am not King Aling's son ...and I am not deserving to be adopted into your family, let alone for you to call me son."

King Lee smiles, "I knew from the very beginning that you were not King Aling's son. His fifteen sons were the ones I found outside the castle. I knew they would fight to their death in attempting to save their father."

The young man looks into King Lee's eyes, but says nothing.

King Lee asks, "You had the chance to escape from me, why did you not? You said you had intended not to return ...so, why did you?"

The young man looks deeply into the king's eyes, "I have never been good at anything. And I am not a good warrior. I returned to

King Aling's side after all the other warriors left, not to console a dying king, but to rob him of his royal robe and crown. It is no fun being a warrior. Even the good ones are not happy. They drink all the time, but they can't wash away the memory of all that blood. I just wanted to imagine I could be happy. I wanted to put on the king's robe and crown to pretend for a while ...to pretend I had a good life. Then you came. I thought you had bought my story ...and I could pretend a bit longer. Then when you called me your son, I felt for that brief moment that my dream could become reality. I wanted so much to be your son. But, now ...it no longer feels good to pretend. Your son would never pretend and deceive."

King Lee persists, "But, you delivered ...and that is something no one else could have done."

The young man insists, "Yes, I told you I devised a plan to save Shannon ...but, instead I'd planned to save myself."

King Lee asks, "So, why didn't you?"

The young man cries with sincerity, "Because when I was no longer pretending, it brought me inescapable misery. My whole life I had been pretending ...and I realized the only thing that ever felt real to me was your love."

King Lee begins to cry, "I didn't understand why—-that at that horrific moment of finding my dear friend, King Aling, and his sons dead—-I felt a very strange mix of anger and rage that I hadn't felt in a very long time. We'd had peace for so long, it felt so very wrong to hate ...yet, it was even scarier how quickly I could be moved to rage. I'd read stories of the past ...of when people did nothing but hate one another. And sure, they all seemed like good reasons ...but it seemed only to bring about bad results. War is often misrepresented ...and used as a tool to dismiss the real reasons people find conflict with one another. Some people say that greed is a major contributing factor for war ...but, I believe the main reason people feel it is worth killing or being killed, is because so many have been taught hate. Hate is an ugly thing ...and war is a natural by-product of it. It is difficult not to hate those who brutally kill those we love, but as war wages on, people fight merely because that is the definition of war. We do what we are taught to do. And war is a condition of either killing, or being killed. So, how can war cease?? It can only cease if individuals can concede that the solution to hate is to cease war. A choice has to be made not to kill. I could have killed you, but I chose not to."

The young man asks, "Why did you choose not to?"

King Lee wipes a tear away, "I've asked myself that many times. I rehearsed many answers in my head ...but, overall I don't really know. As soon as I got word that my own daughter had also been abducted as a result of all the madness, the very hate that I thought was no longer a part of me ...was making a valiant return. My heart was already grieving so much, I was feeling so much anger ...then to hear of Shannon, the fires of rage had been rekindled. I realized that my anger was directed at something that was real ...horrifically real. Yet, it was not hate that I felt ...it was the type of anger that I feel anyone would have felt. It was circumstantial anger, not an all-consuming hate. And I knew that none of that would help me get Shannon back. I was angry ...but, I chose not to hate you. Whatever you were doing, or had done, was only what people of war do. The standard of a good warrior is judged only by the success of accomplishing that which creates the widest spread hatred of others. The greatest warrior does the most killing ...and though the most celebrated by one kingdom, that warrior is most hated by all others. I suppose now, you will be among those who are most hated ...for the humiliation you must have caused them by rescuing Shannon and Ting. You are probably viewed as committing a treasonous act. Why did you risk so much ...for those of us whom you don't really even know?"

The young man cries, "But, I did know what I was looking for, and what I found. I found that I had never felt so important in my entire life ...and I didn't want that feeling to go away. I was overcome *by your acceptance of me. You could have hated me ...but, you chose instead to love me."*

King Lee embraces the young man, "And you chose to love me in return. I want you to stay on ...as my son."

The young man cannot hold back the tears, "Once you accept love, you can't just keep it inside. I must give it as it has been given. I've decided that I must go back. I hope you understand."

King Lee cries, "I beg of you to stay. For you to return ...that would be sure death."

The young man cries, "There is nothing more that I'd like than to stay here with you. But, if I don't risk going back, they will without doubt consider attacking your kingdom next. Without help, they will not stop hating, and the war will continue. But, if I show them the love you've shown me ...love that often takes high risks in the sharing of it, then perhaps I can make a difference in the lives of those who need it the most. It's so easy to hate ...way too easy, but I want them to find love and inner peace, so the war will cease."

The young man is overcome with much emotion. He takes a deep breath, before continuing, "The only hope is for me to try to make a difference ...like you did with me. If I fail, at least I will have tried ...and I can be satisfied with having experienced it. If I die, my wish would be that others would be curious enough to want to know why I was willing to sacrifice, risking everything to help them. Perhaps that would lead people to scratch their heads ...wondering whether I was mad, or whether there was more to it. Perhaps my love will be visible to them ...and they will give up hate too. But, before I am further compelled to stay ...I think I should depart. Please tell Shannon 'goodbye' for me. You have a wonderful daughter. I am so honored, having been able to return her to you. She told me of a very special story ...and before I go, I must say, I agree with her that there is none quite like you, Poppy!"

They embrace again. King Lee doesn't want to let him go, but he knows he must.

* * * * * * * *

(I guess I sort of didn't want to let you go, but I must ...that's it for this series. The series of eight actually began with *'So Loved ...'*)

Well, that series is finished ...but there's more.

Chain-Link Fences
  We Should Also Love One Another
  Who Would Not Want An Inheritance?
  What is His Name?

But wait ...with me there is always more. Yet, you'll have to wait.
  This may take some time, as it involves the input of others.
  The title will be: *'Am I Trying to Take Away From Jesus?'*

Well, that was much quicker than expected ...now, there is also: *'Questions of the Heart'.*

God bless you!!!

(If you want an interesting story for young children, about mice and rats, then there are two written by the Associate Pastor of the church I go to. *'Xavier's Treasures'* and *'Xavier'*—-part two, by Myron Gaul.)

Yes, Myron has been an inspiration and blessing to all of us.